UNPLUGGED

Dedicated to my parents, who are simply the best parents of all time. I am blessed to be your daughter. Thanks for going above and beyond during the writing process.

Thanks, also, to Betsy Flikkema and the rest of the crew at Zondervan for your great work!

www.zonderkidz.com

Unplugged

Requests for information should be addressed to:
Zonderkidz, Grand Rapids, Michigan 49530

Library of Congress Cataloging-in-Publication Data

Crouch, Cheryl, 1968-
Unplugged / by Cheryl Crouch.
p. cm. -- (The Chosen Girls)
Summary: When her father agrees to allow the Chosen Girls to accompany him to Moscow where he has a conference, Trin, excited at the prospect of international exposure, decides this is the perfect opportunity to show Harmony and Mello how a band should be run.
ISBN-13: 978-0-310-71269-5 (softcover)
ISBN-10: 0-310-71269-6 (softcover)
[1. Bands (Music)--Fiction. 2. Rock music--Fiction. 3. Interpersonal relations--Fiction. 4. Moscow (Russia)--Fiction. 5. Russia--Fiction. 6. Christian life--Fiction.] I. Title.
PZ7.C8838Unp 2007
[Fic]--dc22

2006023532

Editor: Bruce Nuffer
Art direction and design: Sarah Molegraaf
Interior composition: Christine Orejuela-Winkelman

Printed in the United States of America

07 08 09 10 11 12 • 7 6 5 4 3 2 1

UNPLUGGED

By Cheryl Crouch

ZONDERVAN.com/
AUTHORTRACKER
follow your favorite authors

You did not choose me, but I chose you and appointed you to go and bear fruit—fruit that will last. Then the Father will give you whatever you ask in my name.
—John 15:16
ROCK
Sweet!
I'm glad we moved to California. I love being close to beaches and mountains. And palm trees are WAY cool ... I still feel like I'm on vacation every time I see one.
Trinity

what to pack:

- super suit
- white boots
- ~~black boots~~
- jeans
- T-shirts for layering
- layered skirt
- high-top boots
- coat!!!
- pink sweater
- ~~green sweater~~
- ~~white sweater~~
- necklaces
- bracelets
- ~~pink lights~~
- white long-sleeve tee
- extra guitar strings
- camera
- ~~books~~
- BIBLE!!!
- bottled water
- blow-dryer

Harmony makes me laugh SO hard!

She is crazy funny, and she will do anything!

rock!

Fundraiser Ideas:

- car wash
- bake sale
- lemonade stand
- cookie dough
- jewelry
- purses

Then the Father will give you whatever you ask in my name.

—John 15:16b

RUSSIA!

This trip is going to be a blast!

It's the chance of a lifetime and I can't wait!!!!!!!

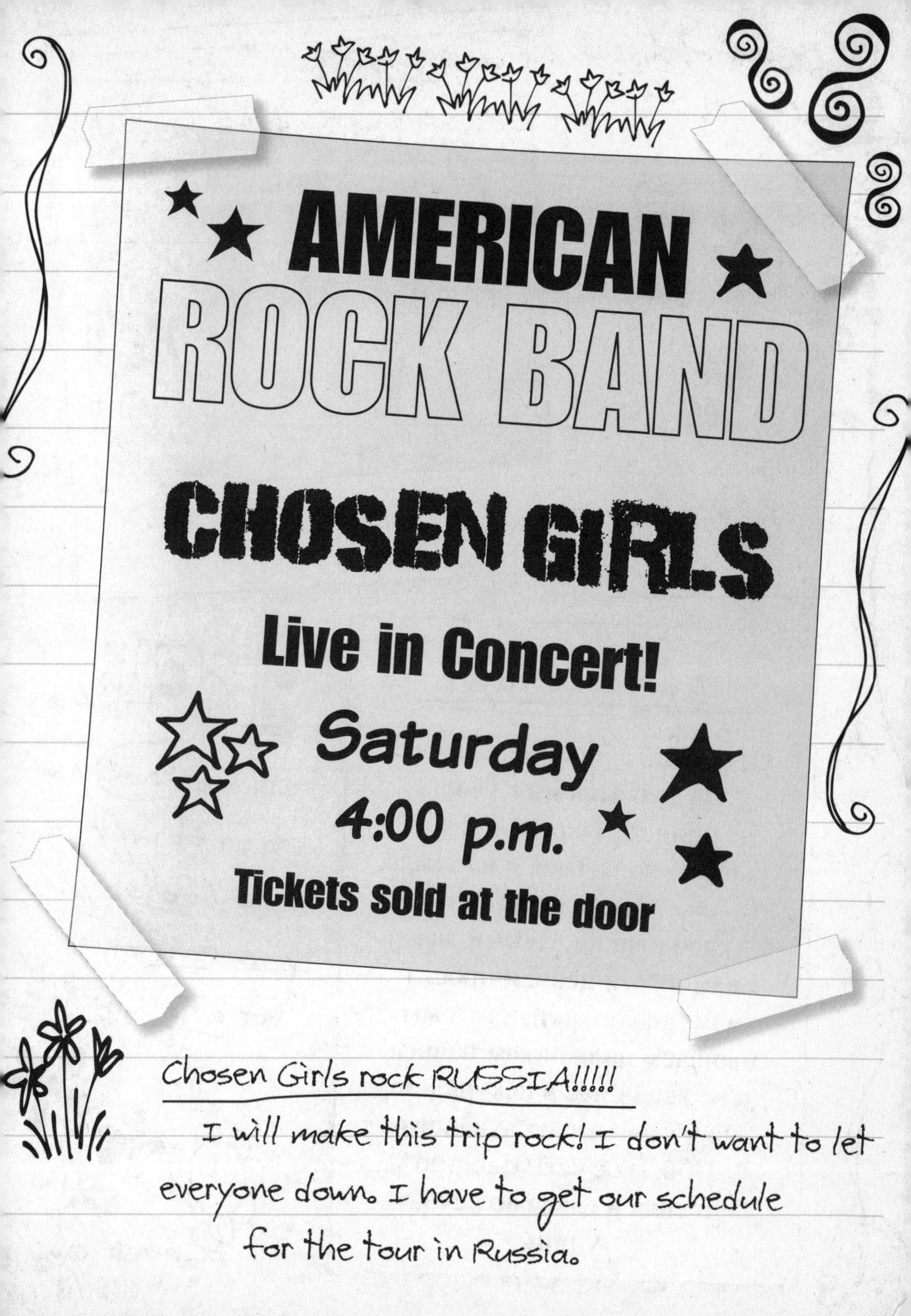
AMERICAN
ROCK BAND
CHOSEN GIRLS
Live in Concert!
Saturday
4:00 p.m.
Tickets sold at the door
Chosen Girls rock RUSSIA!!!!!
I will make this trip rock! I don't want to let
everyone down. I have to get our schedule
for the tour in Russia.

The Lord's Prayer

**Отче наш, сущий на небесах!
Да святится имя Твое;
да приидет Царствие Твое;
да будет воля Твоя и на земле,
как на небе;
хлеб наш насущный дай
нам на сей день; и прости
нам долги наши, как и мы
прощаем должникам нашим;
и не введи нас в искушение,
но избавь нас от лукавого.
Ибо Твое есть Царство
и сила и слава во веки.
Аминь.**

pray

I will ~~love~~ trust you
with all of my heart.
I will follow you
~~the rest of my~~
for all of my life.

I want to be in ~~charge~~ control
but not if it (costs) me my soul
You alone know the path that's best for me
How can I ~~let it~~ give it up?
Trust you to help me ~~know~~ live it up?
You made me—why's that so hard for me to see?

SING*

- [x] bake MORE cookies
- [x] get shots (OUCH!*)
- [x] pack!!! ★
- [x] (finish lyrics)
- [x] call Mello

I wish I could sew like Mello. It would be way fabulous because I could make clothes that aren't like ANYONE else's!

Russian Phrases to learn!

Pozhaluista = Please

Spaseebo balshoye = Thank you very much

Yzumitelno = Marvelous!

kak pazhivayete? = How are you?

Yielding Control to God

love

Western Airlines

Depart: Los Angeles
8:05 a.m.

Arrive: New York
4:55 p.m.

Seat 64 B

0001000101101011011 0000

Western Airlines

Depart: Los Angeles
8:05 a.m.

Arrive: New York
4:55 p.m.

Seat 64 B

0001000101101011011 0000 • 00100011110 1011

This ticket is nontransferable, non-transfundable.

Plane will board 30 minutes prior to take-off.

2 Pcs. of luggage per passenger.

What we've earned so far:

$8 - cookie sale
$250 - jewelry sale
$625 - purses!!!
TOTAL: $883

will trust you
with all of my heart.
I will follow you
for all of my life.
You know the ~~road~~ path ahead
so I will trust you instead
Yeah, I will trust in you!

chapter • 1

•••

Thursday

Moving to California scared me 'cause in Dallas I knew where I fit. I survived some hard lessons in Dallas.

Like when I invited those girls from ballet to my birthday bash. Two of the coolest girls in school — my friends. Then when Ashlyn didn't show and Jade dissed everything we did at the party, I understood. They were only friends if nobody else was around.

I didn't want to start over in California. But when I got here, I met the best friends ever — Harmony and Mello. I stopped worrying about past mistakes. Soon I even quit pretending I had my act together.

Ohwow! We started our own rock band! Music videos and rock concerts. We're actually in them, instead of just watching. Sure, we had challenges, but I just knew I didn't have to worry about being embarrassed anymore.

But I was wrong.
So wrong.

•••

"Give me one more run straight through, and then take five," said the sound engineer over the intercom.

I nodded at him through the huge glass window. The soundman, John, sat in the control room, while Mello, Harmony, and I jammed in studio four. Acoustic tiles, wood, and carpeting covered the floors, walls, and even the ceiling of the room. Our friend Lamont made faces at us behind John's back.

"Sweet! I still can't believe we're in a real recording studio," I said, ignoring Lamont as I quickly fine-tuned my electric guitar.

Mello grinned at me from behind her drum set. "I feel like we live here, after yesterday."

"But how cool is this?" Harmony asked, waving her arms at the microphones, headsets, and glass sound-isolation booths surrounding us. She jerked her head at the control room. "And Lamont looks like he's died and gone to heaven. That control room has enough equipment to launch a space shuttle."

John's voice interrupted us. "Anytime you're ready, Chosen Girls."

Mello tapped three beats and we played the intro. I smiled at Harmony, who played a solid bass line, and then nodded at Mello. We came in on the pickup note:

Oh, Chik'n Quik
Chicken on a stick
It's so yummy for your tummy
Everybody loves Chik'n Quik

Mello's alto blended perfectly with my soprano, and Harmony's bass guitar sounded awesome with my electric. Mello ended the jingle with a cymbal crash. Perfect!

"Thanks," John said. "Take a short break. Be ready to go again in five."

Harmony and I stood our guitars on their stands, and Mello grabbed a bottle of water.

"I can't wait to hear us on the radio!" Harmony said.

Mello laughed. "But ... it's a chicken jingle."

Harmony rounded on her. "Most bands would be psyched to have a manager get them a gig like this. You have to start somewhere."

"But we *have* started," Mello answered. "We're on TV. We do concerts. Why do we need a chicken jingle?"

I giggled as I opened a bottle of juice. I agreed with Mello — it did seem a little lame.

"We need to break into radio," Harmony said in her I'm-trying-to-be-patient-with-you voice. "This is how we're going to do it. Plus, this job got us the hookup for our next concert," she added, digging her hand into a bag of chocolate pretzels and peanuts. "You'll see. Even Makayla and the Snob Mob will forget about our botched show in Lewisville." She flounced to the floor and popped a pretzel in her mouth.

"Makayla and the Snob Mob will always be posers, Harmony," I reminded her. "I thought you figured that out."

Lamont bounded in. "You women sound amazing." He reached for some pretzels. "You sold me. I could eat some chicken on a stick right now!"

The door burst open, and a huge man walked in. "I'm Mr. Walling," he announced in a loud bass voice. "Great studio, huh?"

Harmony put her pretzels behind her and jumped up. "The owner of Chik'n Quik?" She stepped toward him, reaching out her right hand. "I'm Harmony Gomez, manager of the Chosen Girls. I'm the one you spoke to on the phone."

"Glad to meet you, Harmony and Chosen Girls," he boomed, pumping Harmony's arm up and down. "I'm thrilled about our agreement." He seemed to fill the room with his large belly and even larger personality.

"We're ready, sir," John said, sticking his head in the door. He looked at us. "I'm going to play that last recording for Mr. Walling, so you've got a few more minutes of break." He left, and Mr. Walling followed him to the control room.

We could see them talking, but we couldn't hear them through the soundproof glass. They got still, listening. Then Mr. Walling said something. John answered him, and Mr. Walling shook his head. He frowned.

"He didn't like it," Mello whispered.

I watched the discussion, wishing I could read lips but thinking it might be good I couldn't.

"That's normal," I said. "People usually have to record like twenty times to get it right."

Mello tapped nervously on her snare. "I don't think we'll get it any better than that. We aced it."

John leaned over and pushed something, and Mr. Walling's voice filled the room. "Beautiful, just beautiful! I loved it!"

John's voice came next. "I told Mr. Walling he's got the studio for the next four hours, if he wants a few more takes. But he says there's no point."

"Do you have any songs you'd like to record?" Mr. Walling asked. "I've paid for the session, so you might as well use it. And I'd like to listen, if I may."

"Sweet!" I answered. "What first?" I looked at Mello and Harmony, not wanting to waste a second.

" 'You've Chosen Me,' " Harmony said. "Our signature song."

I nodded, and Mello got us started. Something about the studio brought out the best in us. We rocked. We sang "Love Lessons" next. John had us each play individually too.

When our time ran out, Mr. Walling came in and shook our hands. "We'll see you tomorrow at the grand opening," he said.

"Yes, sir," Harmony agreed. "I put your posters all over town."

Mello asked, "What time do you want us there, Mr. Walling?"

Harmony looked sideways at her and answered, "Grand Opening at five, Chosen Girls in place by four. Right?"

"That's right," Mr. Walling agreed.

"And where is your restaurant?" I asked. Harmony frowned at me. "I just want to be sure," I explained. "After your mistake in Lewisville ..."

She glared at me, then turned to Mr. Walling and asked, "The fifteen hundred block of Hibiscus, next to the Wash-and-Run, right?"

Mr. Walling beamed at Harmony. "Just beautiful! I'll see you there." He smiled at all of us. "After what I heard today, I'm even more excited about your concert." He started for the door and added, "Don't forget to listen to the radio. The ad starts running tomorrow." His voice trailed away down the hall. "Beautiful."

John came in as we packed up. "I'll mix and balance these recordings, and you can pick up your CD next week," he told us. "I must say, for a start-up band, you record really well. It takes some groups four days to get a single."

I thanked him, and he said, "That session would usually run you $225 an hour. But don't thank me. Thank Mr. Walling."

As the door closed behind him, Harmony added, "You can also thank your awesome manager. I told you this was a good gig."

•••

Friday

We got to Chik'n Quik at three-thirty on Friday.

"I told you we didn't need to leave straight from school," Harmony griped as she hauled an amp out of Mom's Suburban.

I grabbed another amp. "Hey, better safe than sorry," I responded. "If we want to be a real band, we can't afford to be late. Or go to the wrong location."

"I know the location, Trin," Harmony huffed.

Mello stepped between us. "So Mr. Walling wants us to wear our superhero stuff?" she interrupted. "For the whole concert? Why don't we switch during 'You've Chosen Me,' like we usually do?"

"Yeah," Lamont agreed. "The superhero thing doesn't make sense without the video. It explains where your power comes from."

"I guess I can ask," Harmony answered, heading for the flatbed trailer that would be our stage. "But he wanted to know if we'd be willing to do the whole concert in costume, and I said okay. It seemed like a small thing for what he's paying us. I guess he thinks our super suits are cool."

"Way cool," I said, following her. I put the amp on the edge of the stage and waved an imaginary sword around. "Don't you wish just putting the suit on gave you superpowers?"

"I'd wear mine every day," Harmony agreed with a smile.

Lamont put the soundboard down. "Sorry, women. No power in the suits." He looked around. The stage backed up to a small lawn covered in brilliant green grass, tropical flowers, and palms. To the right, cars cruised by on Hibiscus Drive. "This is a great place for the stage. Right by the main drag. Everyone who passes will know something's going on."

Mello said, "I can't believe I'm doing this."

"It's good for you," I answered. "Little by little, you're overcoming your shyness—breaking out of your shell."

"Little by little?" she asked. "More like you went after my shell with a sledgehammer!"

We got our equipment hooked up and ran through sound checks. Then we grabbed the bags with our costumes in them. "Now, aren't you glad we're early?" I asked. "We have time to get dressed and do our hair."

Mello sighed and said, "Trin, your hair already looks great."

"Same to you, Miss Elegance," I answered with a smile.

Mr. Walling met us on the other side of the parking lot, at the door of Chik'n Quik. His bass voice rang out as he said, "Hello, Chosen Girls. Hello, Lamont! I see you found the stage. Beautiful. Come on in and look around." He held the door for us. "What do you think?"

I looked around. It looked like any other fast-food restaurant. "I . . . uh . . . like the color of your seat covers," I offered.

"Yes, thank you," he answered. "Beautiful."

We headed for the restroom.

Mr. Walling called, "Wait. I have your costumes in the back."

I held up my bag. "No, we've got them here," I corrected. But he was gone.

He came back with a huge box. "Wait till you see these," he said, putting the box on a table. "I ordered three of them from headquarters, and I'm so pleased. You'll stop traffic—no questions asked." He opened the box and reached in.

And pulled out a chicken suit.

•••

Standing onstage, I looked through the hole cut in the beak of my suit. A few cars had already parked, and people laughed and pointed as they came toward us. More and more cars pulled in.

The chicken head I wore was thick enough to be hot, but not thick enough to block the sounds of horns honking on Hibiscus Drive. More than one guy yelled, "Hey, Chicks! Lookin' good!"

Embarrassed, I looked down at my feet. That didn't help. Red chicken claws were there where my ultracool high-heeled boots belonged.

Harmony wisely avoided eye contact. Her bright yellow beak faced straight ahead as we ran through final checks, so I could only see her white feathers and skinny yellow chicken legs.

"At least no one can recognize us." Mello's weak voice came from the direction of her drums, behind me.

I turned to look at her. "Mello, thanks to our overeager manager, signs all over town say 'Chosen Girls to perform at Grand Opening.' Everyone knows it's us."

"So what do you want me to do?" Harmony hissed. "He's paying us. He gave us a free recording session."

Mr. Walling strode across the parking lot toward us, flashing a huge smile and a double thumbs-up. He came onstage and grabbed my microphone.

"Thanks for coming out to our grand opening," he told the gathering crowd. "Please enjoy free samples of our delicious Chik'n Quik chicken on a stick while you listen to the music of the best new group in Southern California: the Chosen Girls!" He turned to us. "Open with the jingle!"

He walked offstage and we started in. I was singing, "It's so yummy for your tummy," when I first saw them in the crowd.

Makayla and the Snob Mob.

•••

After the concert, Mom dropped us at the shed in Mello's backyard. I don't know why we call it the shed. It's more like an apartment or a studio. It's got everything—a couch, TV, plenty of room to jam. It's even decorated with real art and throw pillows that match the curtains.

We unloaded our equipment. But that wasn't all we unloaded.

"Unbelievable!" I shouted at Harmony. "You are the only person who could mess this up so royally." I put my electric down and flopped onto the couch.

"Do you think I enjoyed it?" she yelled back. She threw an armload of extension cords down. "Humiliating myself in front of Makayla and company? *Again!*"

"Forget about the Snob Mob. Half of Hopetown was there," I wailed.

"Look on the bright side," Lamont said, carrying in a drum.

Mello put a snare in the corner and glared at him. "There is no bright side, Lamont."

"But there is," he insisted. "Remember what Trin said before the concert? Based on your costumes today, I'd say Mello isn't the only one who broke out of her shell." He slapped his thigh. "Get it? Chickens? Eggs?"

I rolled my eyes. "So *not* funny, Lamont," I told him. "Harmony, how many times do you expect us to put up with this? I'm not used to being humiliated."

"Stick around," Mello said. "You might *get* used to it."

Harmony looked at me, then at Lamont, and then at Mello. No one said anything.

Harmony blinked and took a deep breath like she didn't want to cry. Then she turned and stomped out.

Lamont followed her.

"I'm with you, Trin," Mello said. "I mean, Harmony's like a sister to me. Has been since second grade. But I can't handle any more of her messes." She sat next to me and put her head in her hands. "What we need is a manager who can actually manage." She looked at me. "I bet you'd be a good manager."

I let out a big breath and shook my head.

•••

Friday Night

We needed to regroup, so we met at Java Joint later.

I apologized to Harmony for my attitude. Mello clued in and said she was sorry too. Lamont didn't make any more smart remarks, and it looked like we would be okay.

Then the Snob Mob came in. Makayla pointed to us and yelled, "Look! My favorite rock band: the Chicken Girls."

Thankfully, they got their drinks to go.

Harmony started bawling. "I'm such a loser. Why do you guys even let me hang with you? I wish ..." She stopped to wipe her nose on her sleeve. "I wish I could just leave the country!"

I looked into her red, swollen eyes and yelled, "That's it!"

They all looked at me.

I flashed them my biggest smile and said, "It's perfect. Exactly what we need. Let's go to Russia!"

chapter • 2

•••

Still Friday Night

They put their drinks down. Lamont said, "Where?"

"Russia," I repeated. "My dad told me last night that he has a conference in Moscow. It's during the next break. Wouldn't it be way fabulous to go with him? Have you guys ever been?"

They looked at me like I had sprouted an extra head.

"To Russia?" Mello asked.

"Yeah," I answered.

"No," she said.

"Nuh-uh," Lamont agreed.

"Me neither," Harmony added. "I haven't been anywhere since we moved here from Peru."

"Ohwow! Let's go!" I said.

Mello shook her head. "We can't just go to Russia," she said.

I prepared to do battle. "Why can't we?" I asked.

Mello looked at Harmony, waiting to be rescued.

Harmony tried. "Russia is, like, a foreign country," she said.

I smiled. "True that, Harmony!" I answered. "And we're free to travel abroad. We're allowed to go to foreign countries."

Mello looked irritated. "It costs money, Trin. And you have to have passports and shots and stuff."

I nodded. "We can raise the money. And it's easy to get passports. Come on! Think of the exciting experiences! We'll make memories to last a lifetime."

Harmony started to smile, and her eyes sparkled. "I've seen pictures of Red Square," she said. "It's *muy bonita*. It would be cool frijoles to get our picture made there."

I wiggled with excitement. "Raise your hand if you'd love to do a concert there. The Chosen Girls on tour in Russia!"

Harmony practically jumped off her chair. "An international tour! Sī! Let's do it!"

I looked at Lamont. "You in? We'll need you on sound."

He grinned. "Sounds good."

We all looked at Mello, who tapped nervously on the edge of the table.

"Mello?" I asked.

The corners of her mouth turned up. "I've always wanted to see St. Basil's Cathedral," she answered.

I jumped up and did a happy dance. I pulled out my cell and punched in Dad's number. When he answered I asked, "Hey, Dad, where are you?"

He was still at work.

"I'm sorry you're having to work so hard," I said. "My buds and I are at Java Joint. Can we bring you a chocolate chip mocha?"

He said sure.

I punched End and walked to the counter. "This is the kind of question you ask in person," I explained.

"And a mocha never hurts," Lamont agreed with a grin.

•••

We walked to the college campus where my dad teaches economics. I love it there—benches tucked into tiny gardens, fountains bubbling, and college students everywhere.

I said hello to Sam, who mans the guard booth, and we started uphill to the business building. The whole time we talked about Russia—what would the food taste like? How would people act?

Our voices echoed in the halls of Dad's building. No one wanted to hang out in the business department on Friday night.

Dad said hello and took a sip of his drink. "So what can I do for you fine folks?" he asked.

"Dad!" I exclaimed. "What makes you think we want anything?"

He laughed. "I don't know. Do you and your friends usually bring me something from Java Joint on Friday nights?"

I looked away. "Yeah, well ..."

Harmony spoke up. "You're a smart man, Mr. Adams. We do want something. We're hoping you can help us with a major cool idea."

Lamont caught Harmony's spirit. "See, sir," he began, "our worldviews are way too limited. There's a whole world out there, and we want to see it."

"You always say traveling is the best education a person can get," I added.

Dad smiled. "Mello, I haven't heard from you. What do you all have in mind? A trip to the beach? A weekend in the mountains?"

Mello said, "Actually, we're hoping you'll take us to Russia."

Dad's face was a riot. Total shock. *"Russia?"*

"You're going anyway," I blurted. "It will be so good for us."

Dad wiped his face with one big hand. Then he smiled.

"You're right," he said. "I'd love to take you."

Mello squealed. Harmony and I screamed and jumped up and down. Lamont said, "Oh, happy day!"

"On one condition," Dad continued.

We stopped celebrating.

Dad looked each of us in the eyes, like he was measuring how serious we were. Then he said, "You raise your own money for airfare and meals."

I sighed in relief. "Well, yeah. No biggie."

Everyone looked at me, surprised. "I mean, yeah, it's big," I stammered. "But we can do it."

"It's crazy, but I really think you can," Dad agreed, nodding.

•••

"We already have the money from the chicken jingle and the chicken concert," I said as we started walking back.

"Aha!" Lamont said. "A bright side at last."

"And raise your hand if you think a bake sale would be fun," I asked. "We could sell cookies. I've got this recipe for Simply Scrumptious Triple Chunk— "

Lamont interrupted to ask, "Do you know how many cookies you're talking about?"

"Hush, Lamont, I want to hear about the triple-chunk stuff," Harmony said. She turned to me, her eyes bright.

I ignored Harmony and answered Lamont. "I didn't say it would be our *only* fund-raiser. I said it would be our first."

"I've seen people sell stuff in front of the grocery store," Mello offered. "You know, set up a card table and a little sign—"

"Or the college campus!" I said. "College kids are always half-starved. Especially for homemade food."

We got to my house. "Come on. I bet we have enough stuff in the kitchen to make a double batch. We can start tonight, make more in the morning, and sell all afternoon. Our next $200 will be in the bag by tomorrow night."

Mello paused by the front door. "Um, my parents don't even know about the trip yet," she pointed out.

I patted her on the shoulder. "Minor detail. Bake now, explain later."

"It's getting late, Trin," Lamont said as he looked at his watch.

I handed him my cell then opened the door. "So call home. Tell them you're making cookies at my house."

"I'll help if I can lick the bowl," Harmony volunteered as they followed me inside.

"I've heard Russians love Americans," I said as I dug out the recipe. "When a friend of mine went, so many people came to see them they had to stand in the aisles and look in through windows. And they were just a church choir. Imagine what they'd do for a real live rock band!" I opened the pantry and pulled out cocoa, flour, and chocolate chips.

"Oh, yeah," Lamont said. "How about if I record the whole trip? And all your concerts."

"Sweet!" I said, setting the sugar and vanilla next to the other stuff on the counter.

Mello shook her head. "I'm not sure I'm ready for you to pick up that camera again, Lamont!"

Harmony messed with the measuring cups. "Wait. You are so getting ahead of yourselves," she huffed. "What are you thinking? We're just going to walk around in a foreign country and pull out our guitars and drums and do concerts anywhere we feel like it? As manager, I happen to know it's not that easy."

I bit my lip. Then in a calm, controlled voice I said, "I haven't worked out the details yet, Harmony. But I will. And it's going to be a trip you'll never forget. I promise."

•••

Saturday

The next morning, we set up near the college cafeteria. "This way they can buy our cookies for dessert," I explained.

Lamont popped out the legs on the card table. "I never want to see chocolate again," he complained. "How many triple chunks did we make?"

I lifted a box of cookies onto the table. "Each batch makes forty-eight cookies. We made eight batches, so that's . . ."

"Three hundred eighty-four cookies," Harmony said with a moan, flopping onto a folding chair.

"No, we made three hundred fifty-four," Mello corrected.

Harmony grabbed a pen and paper. She wrote out the problem and held it up for us to see. "Three hundred *eighty-four*," she said triumphantly.

Mello grinned at her. "It was three hundred eighty-four before *you* started eating the dough. You must have eaten at least thirty cookies' worth."

Two surfer dudes wandered by.

"Want some homemade cookies?" I called.

They walked over to the table. "Do you take debit cards?" one asked.

"No, only cash," Harmony said with a smile.

"Sorry. Don't have any cash on me," he said. "You?" he asked his buddy.

"Nope. Wish I did." They left.

The campus was strangely quiet.

"Where are all the starving college kids you told us about?" Harmony asked.

I shrugged my shoulders. "I don't know. They're usually everywhere. I've never seen the campus so dead."

"First time here on a Saturday?" Lamont asked. I nodded. "Bet everyone went home for the weekend," he said.

I looked at our boxes and boxes of cookies, wondering if we should pack up and go home. But just then, four girls walked by. "Want cookies?" I asked.

"Simply Scrumptious Triple Chunk Fudge," Harmony added.

They practically ran over us. They squealed, "Cookies!" and "Chocolate!" and each bought two.

"Our first four dollars," Lamont said proudly. "Moscow, here we come!"

• • •

"Four measly dollars," Harmony complained hours later as we packed up. "I can't believe we stayed up half the night baking *and* got up early to bake *and* sat here all day and only sold eight cookies. We spent more than four dollars on ingredients."

"So, actually, we lost money," Mello pointed out.

I sighed. "We didn't quite reach our goal," I admitted.

"Reach our goal?" Lamont said. "Woman, we didn't even get on the track. We're not in the ballpark. Nowhere near the playing field — "

"I get it, Lamont," I interrupted, shoving a triple chunk in his mouth. "Be quiet and eat a cookie."

chapter • 3

• • •

Sunday Afternoon

I lay on my bed, staring at the boxes of Simply Scrumptious Triple Chunks stacked around my room. I sighed, got up slowly, and got a cookie out. I raised it to my mouth ... and almost gagged.

I couldn't make myself eat even one more.

I had been so sure about the bake sale. The way all of us worked together in the kitchen—way cool. We laughed the whole time, planning and dreaming about Russia. And then the whole sale flopped. *Four dollars!* Now what? Would they trust me to plan anything after this? Three hundred forty-six cookies might go stale, but I had to keep plans for the trip fresh.

I felt like those dumb boxes were laughing at me. I stuck my tongue out at them. But it ended up being the boxes of cookies that gave me my way fabulous idea.

I picked up my cell. "Harmony, emergency meeting in the shed at three o'clock. I'll call Lamont. You call Mello, OK?"

They all showed. "OK, everybody," I began. I clicked on my new PDA and found the agenda I had typed in. "We need to raise thousands of dollars, fast. For normal people, it would be impossible. But not for us!"

"Especially since we've already raised four dollars," Harmony said in her snottiest voice.

"We're about to make a lot more," I said quickly. "Get this: we sell the cookies to Lottie for fifty cents each. She can sell them at Java Joint for a buck apiece. She wins, we win."

"So if she says yes, we get . . . what? Almost two hundred dollars?" Mello asked. "We need thousands, Trin."

"Good point," I agreed. "But that was only phase one. Phase two: we use some of the profits to buy stuff for a car wash."

Harmony interrupted to ask, "Lamont, doesn't your mom sell stuff on the Internet?"

He nodded. "That's right."

"Do you think she'd get us a hookup to do that?"

"I bet she would."

I interrupted. "That sounds way fabulous, but there's a problem. I don't see people buying these cookies over the Internet. Why not sell them to Lottie?"

"Not cookies," Harmony said. "Something else. Like jewelry! I've got loads already made up, and it won't take long to make more."

Mello actually looked excited. She clapped her hands and said, "Excellent. It's so beautiful! We could charge lots for it!"

Harmony's face lit up. "Mello, what about those hot purses you've been making? Could you make more?"

Mello smiled. "They're way easy."

"Cool frijoles!"

I was losing control of the meeting, fast. I said, "But what about—"

Lamont interrupted. "I can set up a site for the Chosen Girls. I'll tell about the band and the trip, and show photos of the stuff you're selling. I could even sell the *You've Chosen Me* DVDs. And those new CDs, when they're ready."

Harmony jumped up and started dancing. "Oh yeah, oh yeah. Chosen Girls rock the World Wide Web."

"Let's head next door," Lamont said. "We have no time to lose."

Harmony and Mello followed him to the door without glancing at me.

I wanted to yell after them, *Excuse me. Who is in charge of this meeting? Who thought of this trip? Who invited all of you?*

Instead I mumbled, "So no one cares about all these Simply Scrumptious Triple Chunks?"

Harmony stopped and turned around. "Sí, I care. Why don't you bring a batch to Lamont's house?"

Then she was gone.

I punched the power button on my PDA, shutting off all my great ideas, and followed her.

•••

Monday

The next afternoon I sat in the shed trying to follow Harmony's directions. I am *not* all about making jewelry.

"No, Trin, it's purple, green, blue, green, purple," she said for the fifth time.

It didn't matter, because right then I dropped one end of the string. The beads I'd been threading for the last ten minutes poured onto the carpet.

Mello looked up from the sewing machine she had carried out to the shed and giggled. "Or you could do purple, purple, blue, green, purple, green, green, blue," she said, calling out the colors around my feet.

I growled and squatted down, picking the beads out of the carpet.

"Would you rather help me with the purses, Trin?" she asked.

I would rather do my own thing, I thought. *I'm sick of helping everyone else with* their *great ideas*.

I dumped the beads in the little holder.

Harmony yelled, "Trin! Don't put them all in the same box. You have to divide them by color."

I clenched my teeth together and started sorting beads. "Sure, Mello," I mumbled. "Tell me how to make purses."

•••

The Next Thursday

On Thursday, we sat in the school cafeteria, eating lunch at our regular table.

"Raise your hand if you think it's amazing that just one week ago tomorrow I had the big idea," I said.

Mello looked at me and said, "What idea?"

"Hello! Only the idea for the Chosen Girls to go to Russia," I answered, not believing I had to remind her.

"Oh, yeah," she said with a nod. "It's just that we've done so much since then, I forgot who first brought it up."

You and everyone else, I thought.

"We're really going. Cool frijoles!" Harmony squealed. Then she lowered her voice. "I'm excited but I'm a little nervous. What if something bad happens over there—like what if one of us gets sick? Some hospitals still don't have much medicine."

"Why don't we bring some?" Mello asked.

"My mom always packs a first-aid kit," I explained. "She's a world-class traveler. We've been all over—"

"Not for us, Trin," Mello interrupted. "For the hospitals. We could ask people to donate supplies like bandages and aspirin. Maybe even little toys for kids. Now, that would be excellent."

"Sí," Harmony said. "My mamma knows a couple of nurses. She could talk to them."

"And Dad knows every doctor in town, I bet," Mello added. "And he's friends with the manager of that toy store on Main Street."

"Nice thought, but I doubt we can pull it off," I said, shaking my head. "We'll have our instruments and soundboard and amps ..."

"But we're allowed two suitcases each, right?" Harmony asked.

"We could each fill our second suitcase with hospital supplies and toys!" Mello said.

"I don't know anyone with a toy store. Or any doctors or nurses," I complained. "No one in our family has even been sick since we moved here."

Mello patted my hand. "Don't worry, Trin. I'll fill your suitcase for you."

•••

"Do you think you can keep up with demand?" Lamont asked. "This is craziness!"

I reached for the papers he held, but he handed one to Harmony and one to Mello.

Nothing for me.

Harmony looked at her sheet. "A hundred and five necklaces?" she asked.

Mello looked up from her paper and said, "Ninety-four purses?"

Lamont nodded. "And the site hasn't been up a week!"

I looked at their shocked faces and crossed my arms. In a voice full of triumph I declared, "I told you the Internet wasn't a good idea."

"Not a good idea?" Harmony echoed. "Are you *loco*? We're making ten dollars off every necklace and every purse. Don't you see? We've made two thousand dollars in less than a week!"

"But you have to make over a hundred necklaces and purses," I reminded her.

"Sī, we're going to be very busy," she agreed, handing me a box of beads. "Get stringing."

chapter:4

• • •

Wednesday, One Week Later

That next Wednesday I text-messaged the band and Lamont invitations for a Russian theme party in the shed. I didn't spill the real reason for the party: I had just gotten some great news. I hoped I could wait until Friday to tell them.

I spent the next two days printing out pictures of stuff from Russia, and posters of the Russian words for *thank you* and *you're welcome*. I even found a CD of Russian music and some Russian-language CDs.

• • •

Friday

I got to the shed early Friday and got everything set up — the posters on the wall and the music in the CD player. When

Harmony and Mello came, I handed them each a scarf. "We're going to tie them on our heads like babushkas," I explained, putting mine on and knotting it under my chin. I batted my eyelashes at them and smiled. "Am I stunning?"

"Just ravishing," Mello said in a sarcastic voice. She held her scarf by one corner, like it had slime on it or something. "Do we have to wear these in Russia?"

"No, Mello," I answered, trying to keep my voice sweet. "It's just for tonight. And it's supposed to be fun."

She finally grinned and put it on. "I guess it's better than turning my hair blue," she said. "I think I'll forget to take that blue stuff with me to Russia."

"No way," I said. "Blue hair is your trademark now. You aren't getting out of it, so you might as well give up."

Lamont knocked and then walked in. He looked at the three of us in our scarves and held his hand out to me.

I laughed.

He said, "What? I don't get a scarf?"

"You need one of those huge fur hats," Harmony said.

Lamont nodded and walked immediately to the hot dogs. "I'll have to get me one of those."

When everybody had their food I said, "Ohwow, do I have some news."

"I've got a scoop too," Lamont said.

"What? What is it?" Harmony asked.

Lamont looked at me and said, "You go first."

I folded my hands together and took a deep breath. "Well, I wrote the man in charge of my dad's conference. I told him all about the Chosen Girls — how we're a new band and we've won a contest and we're on TV and all. And — this is so *sweet*—he got us a hookup with someone near Ukraine who'll set up a tour!"

I waited for them to scream with joy, but they didn't.

Mello just said, "That's good. What will we be touring out there?"

I laughed. "Not that kind of tour. I mean, I'm sure we'll tour Moscow, and we'll tour the Kremlin and all. But I'm saying this man will set up a tour for *us*—a concert tour. It's official: the Chosen Girls, on tour in Russia!"

Lamont said, "Oh, happy day! I knew you'd pull it off, Trin. And I'm pumped to be on sound."

Mello sighed and said, "I guess this means I have to take my drums. I don't see how I'm going to get them there."

"Oh, quit, Mello," Harmony told her. "This will rock. Cool frijoles, Trin!"

I beamed at them.

Then Harmony said, "So do I need to do anything special—you know—as band manager?"

My heart almost stopped. That's all I needed—Harmony messing things up on an international scale. I said, "Um, not just yet. I mean, I think I can handle it. For now, anyway. I'll . . . let you know." I looked around, desperate to change the subject. My eyes fell on Lamont, who sat devouring his fourth hot dog. "So, Lamont, what's your news?"

He chewed and grinned at the same time. His eyes lit up and he started nodding. Still chewing, he gave us a thumbs-up and wiggled his eyebrows up and down.

"Oh, please, Lamont," Mello griped. "Just swallow your food and tell us already!"

He kept us waiting a minute more. Finally he swallowed. "Someone really liked the website, and they offered to match any funds we raise," he announced with a smile. "Based on what we've raised so far—if this guy comes through—we'll have enough!"

"Who would do that?" I asked. "Who would give us that much money?"

"He said to call him Mr. Smith Number One," Lamont answered.

"From the concert!" Harmony shrieked. "That concert we did at the wrong park. What a man!"

"Excellent," Mello agreed. "Maybe something good came from that disaster. I still say I've never been so embarrassed in my life. Even the chicken suits weren't that bad. When we found out hundreds of people waited at that other park ..."

"Ohwow, yes. And meanwhile, we did our whole show for—what?—eight people?" I asked.

Lamont patted Harmony's back and said, "So anyway, Mello's right. Something good has come out of it."

I noticed Harmony looked like she might cry. I guess since the whole thing had been her mistake, she was maybe a little sensitive about it. I decided to help her out. "This is great news," I said, grabbing another handful of chips. "And just in time, because we leave in a week."

Harmony looked a little more relaxed.

"I got a little something for each of you," I said, grabbing a big gift bag. I reached in, pulled out a CD, and handed it to Harmony. She got all happy ... until she looked at the cover.

" 'Learn Russian in Ten Days,' " she read. "Um ... *gracias*."

I handed Mello and Lamont theirs. "These are way fabulous. But we don't have quite ten days, so you'll need to double up on a few lessons. Now, do you guys have any questions about traveling overseas?" I asked.

Mello made a face. "Wait. How much Russian can we really learn now? Isn't it a little late?"

"Every word you learn will be one more than you knew before," I pointed out. "People in other countries love it when you speak their language. Even if it's not perfect."

Harmony jumped up and smiled at me. "I bet you're right, Trin," she said.

I smiled back, glad to see her catch my excitement.

"And if they like us to speak it, they'll *love* for us to sing it," she said. "Let's search the Net and find a Russian song we can learn. Lamont, we need your machinery." She started for the door.

"But I had more to tell you," I sputtered.

She looked back. "Tell us while we're choosing a song to learn."

•••

We found a website and listened to songs in Russian, but we couldn't tell for sure what they said. Then Lamont found a copy of the Lord's Prayer written out in Russian characters—*and* spelled out phonetically.

"You could sing this!" he said. "People sing the Lord's Prayer at weddings and stuff."

Harmony stood up and sang in a superhigh opera voice (it wasn't pretty): " 'Our Father in heaven, hallowed be your name.' "

Mello walked to the screen. She mimicked Harmony, but sang the Russian words. "Oht-chee nosh, soos-shee nah nyeh-byeh-sahkh dah svyah-teet-syah eem-yah Tvah-yoh."

She ran out of notes with four syllables left, so she sang them all on the same note, without taking a breath, and then died laughing. "I think we're going to need a new tune!"

Harmony looked at me. "That's your job, Trin," she said.

"The Lord's Prayer is long!" I complained. "It's going to be hard to learn. What if we mess up?"

Harmony crossed her arms and said, "Trin, the Russians will love that we're trying. Even if it's not *perfect*."

I gave her a little smirk.

Mello cleared her throat and said, "So before we figure out the music, what else did you want to tell us, Trin?"

"Well," I said, "the main thing to remember on the trip is to be flexible. Things don't always go like you expect them to when you're traveling in a foreign country. You have to be ready to go with the flow."

They nodded.

I added, "It's also good to call things 'different' instead of 'weird.' Like food, the way people act, whatever. Don't assume something's bad just because it's different from what we do here. Because believe me, it will be different."

•••

The Next Thursday

I stayed up late the night before the trip rearranging my suitcase. Since we had decided to fill our second suitcases with medical supplies and toys, I really didn't have room to spare. I finally got the perfect combos, so I could switch tops, pants, and skirts to make enough outfits to last the trip.

•••

Friday

The next morning I jumped out of bed when the alarm went off. Finally!

We grabbed Pop-Tarts and loaded our bags into the Suburban.

We had to drop off my little brother, Tucker, and then Dad wanted to stop by campus.

I asked, "What for?"

"I need to grab stamps out of my desk so I can mail these bills," he answered.

I looked at my watch. "Couldn't we do it when we get home?"

Dad said, "That depends. Do you want to have running water and electrical service when we get back? Besides, the tickets are in my desk, so I have to go to my office."

I sighed loudly.

We got there, and Dad said Mom and I could wait in the car, because he'd only be a minute. But I couldn't handle just sitting, so I followed him in. He pulled stuff out of his desk and started sticking stamps on envelopes. Then he turned on his computer.

"Dad, what are you doing?" I asked, really afraid now. "Don't start a project on the computer. We'll never catch the plane."

"I'm not starting a project. I'm setting up an automatic out-of-office reply in case anyone emails while I'm gone. That's it. It takes less than two minutes. We're not going to miss our flight."

"But, Dad, we so need to be the first ones there. I have to walk Harmony and Mello through security and stuff. They're probably already at the airport waiting for us. They don't know what to do."

Dad typed away, ignoring me. I looked around for something I could do to speed things up. I saw the bills stacked on Dad's desk. I scooped them up and said, "I'll go stick these in the mail drop and wait in the car."

I walked to the official blue mailbox on the corner and dropped the letters in. Then I climbed in the car with Mom. True to his word, Dad came out a minute later. I sighed with relief when he started the car, and we headed toward the airport.

We were about ten minutes down the road when Mom said, "Jeff, I'd like to look at the itinerary."

Dad said, "Sure," and patted his shirt pocket. Then his pants pocket. Then his other pants pocket.

Mom said, "Very funny, Jeff. It's with the tickets, right?"

And Dad said, "Yes, it's with the tickets. And I wish I was joking. Check my briefcase."

He drove while Mom dug. Then he suddenly swung onto the shoulder of the highway and stopped the car. He stared straight ahead. I could see his hands squeezing the steering wheel so hard his knuckles turned white.

He said, "Trin, when you picked up the bills off my desk, are you sure you only got bills?"

I felt my stomach turn over. "I think so, Dad."

"This isn't a time to think so, Trin. I have to know. Is it possible that you picked up our tickets as well? Do you maybe have them in the backseat?"

I actually looked around as if they might miraculously appear, even though I knew I hadn't brought them into the Suburban. "They aren't back here, Dad," I finally said.

Dad turned to Mom. "Let's go back. Maybe they're still in my desk."

But I could tell from his voice he knew they weren't.

"What are you saying, Jeff?" Mom asked in a shaky voice. "What do you think happened to our tickets?"

Dad breathed real deeply as he exited the highway. Then he said, "I think Trin put them in the mail drop."

I swallowed. No way. I had been trying to speed things up by mailing the bills. Mailing our tickets would so not speed anything up.

"But how can we get them out?" Mom asked.

"We can't. It's against federal law to tamper with the mail. Besides, it's impossible to get something out of those mail drops." Dad pulled up to a light and signaled to go under the highway and head back to his office.

I felt hot tears start to run down my cheeks. We were going to miss the whole trip, and it was my fault.

Then Mom said, "Wait a minute! Do we even need tickets? Can't they find us by our drivers' licenses these days?"

"Not for flights to Russia, no. We have to have those tickets."

We pulled back into the parking lot at Dad's office. He went inside to look, and Mom and I ran to the mailbox.

"Ohwow, whoever invented these things must have been way smart," I said as I pushed and pulled the handle. "Dad's right. There's no way to get inside there." I kicked the bottom, hoping the whole thing might just fall over. *Ouch!*

"It's even stronger than it looks," I told Mom. "Raise your hand if you wish we had a blowtorch in the car."

"Blowtorching our tickets and other people's mail isn't the answer. I hope he finds the tickets in his office," Mom said in a clipped voice, "or I don't know what we'll do." She wrapped her arms around herself, kinda like she wanted to give herself a hug.

I stepped toward her, but then I stopped. It was my fault she was upset. She probably didn't want a hug from me. We hadn't even left Hopetown, and I'd already ruined the whole trip.

Dad came out of the office and I thought, *Please let him be carrying tickets!*

I looked at his hands.

Nothing.

Dad said, "They have to be in the drop, and we can't get them out. All I can think is to pray that God will show us what to do."

We bowed our heads right there on the corner and Dad prayed. After he said, "Amen," he looked up and started running.

I thought, *Ohwow, now Dad's lost it. He thinks he can run to Russia.*

Then I saw why he was running. A mail carrier! On the next block!

Dad ran right up to the mail truck and started talking to the carrier. Then the little truck headed our way. Dad jogged along behind it.

The driver pulled up next to us. "So you've got a little problem, eh?" he said, jumping out of the truck. "It's a good thing it happened now. This is my route, so I can open the box."

He unlocked the box and found our tickets. He held them out but didn't release his grip as Dad latched on to them.

"Wait a minute," the mailman said, eyeing the papers with a grin. "Three tickets to Russia? I said I'd get them out, but I didn't say I'd give them to you. Maybe I should take a little vacation."

For just a second, I thought Dad's head might implode. But the mailman burst out laughing and handed them over. We piled back into the car before we finished thanking him.

• • •

By the time we fought LA traffic, parked, got our shuttle, and waited through crazy-long security lines, I thought I would have at least five heart attacks. The Dallas airport is huge, but LAX is a monster. We ran to our gate—my little carry-on wheels *click*, *click*, *click*ing on the tiles behind me.

I saw it first and yelled, "Gate 12!"

But no one stood in line. The place was empty.

They had already boarded the plane.

chapter • 5

• • •

Friday

It couldn't be. How could we send Harmony, Mello, and Lamont to Russia all alone? They'd never make it!

I noticed a smiling attendant standing by the door. Then, through the huge glass windows, I saw the plane behind her.

Our plane. It hadn't left yet.

I rushed up and handed the worker my boarding pass. I said, "Raise your hand if you thought we missed it. Thank you for still being here! Ohwow, we just had to make this flight. My friends are on the plane, and they've never been overseas. They're counting on me—I'm in charge of the whole trip!"

She reached behind me for Mom's pass and said, "Then you better get onboard. We'll be shutting the door soon."

I ran down the little tunnel, flashed a huge smile at the next attendant, went in, and looked for my seat.

Harmony and Mello yelled, "Trin! Where were you?"

I pushed my bag under my seat and said, "Ohwow, don't even ask."

That's when I noticed Lamont, with his video camera on and pointed at me. He said, "No, really, Trin. Tell us the whole story. We've got plenty of time."

My dad rescued me. He looked at a man two rows back and said, "Hey, Tom! Good to see you. It's been a couple of years." He walked back and shook the man's hand.

"Good to see *you,*" Tom answered. "Thought you were going to miss the flight. This is my son, Joel."

I looked from the man to his son and stopped breathing.

Everything about Joel—wavy honey-blond hair, high cheekbones, shoulders so wide they hardly fit in the seat—was totally magazine model. He glanced up, oh-so-casually, and nodded at Dad. I wanted to do something, anything, to turn those gray-green eyes my direction.

Dad said, "I didn't realize you planned to bring your son. Let me introduce you to my wife and daughter."

Sweet!

Oh, yeah. Gray-green eyes looking at me. I felt myself drowning.

"You're going all the way to Moscow?" Harmony blurted. She stepped into the aisle, right between me and Joel. I stood behind her, a silent idiot, wiping my mouth every once in a while to check for drool.

"Where are you from?" Harmony asked.

"Bakersfield," he answered. The corners of his mouth turned up in an amazing grin. "My dad teaches economics there. That's why he's going to this conference."

"So what are you gonna do while your dad's in meetings?" Harmony asked.

He shrugged and grinned a little bigger. "Watch a lot of Russian TV?" Those gorgeous eyes finally wandered from Harmony's face. He looked at me and asked, "What will you be doing during the conference?"

"Our band is doing a tour near Ukraine," Harmony answered before I could say a word.

He looked impressed. "You have a band?"

I didn't give Harmony a chance. I said, "We're called the Chosen—"

"Please take your seats and place them in their upright, locked position. Fasten your seat belts and put your tray tables up," the intercom blasted.

"Girls," I finished, before I groaned and walked back to my seat. Then Harmony and Mello both wanted to sit by a window, so we had to do one last shuffle. We ended with Harmony by a window and Lamont beside her. I sat next to Mello in the row behind them.

While the plane taxied, I wondered why Harmony needed a window. She spent the whole time looking back through the crack between the seats, pretending to talk to us but staring at Joel.

When the plane picked up speed, she finally turned around. Mello pressed her face against the glass, and I peeked around her to watch the airport buildings whiz past.

As we lifted off, Mello reached over and grabbed my hand, squeezing it hard. I knew how she felt. The force of takeoff pressed me against my seat, and I said a little prayer. (Liftoff and landing are the only parts of flying I don't like.)

"Look! You can see the big LAX letters!" Harmony called. "And those tall pylon things outside the airport."

"But they don't look big from here. And the cars look like toys!" Mello said. Then she gasped. "The Pacific! It's beautiful!"

We stared out the windows until our world disappeared, and a blanket of bumpy white clouds replaced it. Then we stared a little longer. "Doesn't it look like you could roll on them?" Harmony asked.

"OK, time to get our heads out of the clouds," I said, reaching under my seat for my bag. "Did you all listen to the Russian-language CDs I gave you?"

They looked down and shook their heads.

"That's what I thought," I said, pulling stuff out of my little suitcase. "But don't worry. I'm all over it." I handed a player to Mello, then Harmony. "I brought all of our old portable players and copies of the CD." I gave Lamont his and put mine on my lap. I flashed them a big smile and said, "This flight is a perfect time to learn the language. And remember what I told you about jet lag. You need to try to sleep at least four hours on the plane—either this flight or the next one."

Harmony squirmed around in her seat. "Impossible! How could anyone sleep jammed into a tiny space like this?" Her eyes darted behind us, to Joel. "I feel sorry for great big guys," she said.

"That's sweet, but don't worry about me," Lamont said, flexing his nonexistent muscles. "I can sleep anywhere."

Harmony rolled her eyes, put her earphones on, and started her CD. She leaned her head back, closed her eyes, and yelled, "Thank you. *Spah-see-bah.*"

The man in the seat in front of her turned around and glared. Mello, still trying to figure out her own CD, leaned up to Harmony and asked, "Why are you yelling?"

Harmony said, "What? I can't hear you! This Russian CD is too loud. No. *Nyet.* I can't hear."

I reached over the seat, pulled one of her earphones away from her ear, and said, "Turn it down, Harmony. You're blasting the whole plane."

She smiled and adjusted her volume. "I'll do that. Yes. *Dah.* I'll turn it down."

Harmony didn't make it too far past please and thank you. She fell asleep leaning against the window, and Mello fell asleep leaning on me.

I needed to make a trip up the aisle, but I couldn't stand to wake up Mello. So I waited. And practiced saying, "Where is the restroom, please?" in Russian.

By the time the plane touched down in New York, every muscle in my body hurt. My face felt greasy and my eyes were bleary, but I had a job to do. "Ohwow, I wish we had time to shop New York City! Unfortunately, we've only got 45 minutes till our next plane takes off," I announced before the little bell dinged. "We're landing at terminal 2, and we take off from terminal 6. I've studied the airport map, and I know where our gate is. As soon as you can get off the plane, follow me."

We waited by the gate until I saw Joel come out. I flashed him a smile and started leading the way across JFK—another of the biggest airports in the world. We rushed past people in bright Indian saris, embroidered African dresses, classic business suits, and baggy gangsta clothes. I found the Airtrain and we crowded on. I tried not to faint when Joel grabbed the same pole I was holding onto and grinned down at me.

"Aren't we supposed to take a *plane*?" Harmony asked as we left the terminal and rode a rail climbing higher and higher off the ground. "What are we doing on a train?"

Joel shifted his attention to Harmony and laughed. "This airport is huge. This thing gets us from one terminal to another. Then we find our gate."

"So we have to walk even more?" Harmony whined. "I wish I had a rolling bag like Trin's."

"When you travel as much as I do, you know wheels can be your best friend," I explained.

Joel looked at Harmony's backpack. "Is that all you've got? I can carry that," he offered.

Her eyes got huge. "Would you? Thanks!" she gushed.

I looked down at my bag and kicked it. "Stupid wheels," I muttered.

We got off at terminal 6, and they followed me to gate 24. I checked my watch as we walked up and smiled in relief. Then I read the sign over the desk: Flight 346 to Tokyo.

Tokyo?

I turned to the group, panicked. "They must have changed the gates! We only have 17 minutes left. What if it's in a different terminal?"

Lamont shook his head and pointed at the next gate. I squinted and read the sign: Flight 2148 to Moscow. I smiled and said, "Uh, yeah. Tricked ya!" and dashed to gate 25.

On the plane, Joel switched seats with the woman next to Lamont. The two guys totally hit it off.

"Come on tour with us, Joel," Lamont said. "Defend me from these women, I beg you!"

Joel looked at us and laughed. "I can only imagine how hard it is for you, Lamont, surrounded by gorgeous rock stars."

We giggled, but I knew my face must be bright red.

"I'd be giving up a lot. I hear Russian TV is way cool ..." Joel looked at the ceiling of the plane, like he really had to think about it. "But how often does a guy get to tour Russia with a rock band? I'm in!"

I sat back in my seat and tried not to smile too big. Over a week of looking at Joel—way fabulous.

After the flight attendants served dinner, they turned down the lights in the plane and asked everyone to close their window shades. They passed out pillows and blankets and even those little sleep masks. I put one on, and crashed.

In the middle of a great dream about Joel and me singing a duet in Russian, I heard a voice say something about landing. I forced my eyes open.

•••

Saturday Around Noon

And woke up just in time for touchdown in Moscow. Sweet!

I couldn't wait to get off the plane. But of course I had to. I don't know why it takes everyone so long to grab a carry-on and walk off the plane. Mello, Harmony, and I stood in the aisle, waiting for people to get out of the way.

Lamont said, "You might as well sit down and relax, women. We're not going anywhere for a while."

Joel said, "He's right." He wove his fingers together, stretched his arms over his head, and yawned.

"But we're in Russia!" I told them. "We have places to see and concerts to give. I want to get out there! I want to see Red Square! I want to hug a babushka!"

Harmony shook her head. She said, "The Russian grandmothers I've seen in pictures don't look like they want to be hugged, Trin."

I smiled. "They just need some love, Harmony," I answered.

"You probably got that right, Trin," Joel said. "A hug never hurt anyone."

I spun around to face him, but he was looking right over my head at Harmony. I felt my face flush.

"Sure," I muttered, wishing I could disappear until we finally got off the plane.

•••

We made it through customs and dragged our gear outside, where a blast of cold air greeted us. I buttoned up my coat and announced, "First stop: Red Square."

Lamont pointed to our pile of luggage. Between our bags of clothes, our bags of medical supplies, and all the band's equipment, it looked crazy-huge. "I don't think so, Trin," he said. "We need to get rid of this stuff first."

Dad agreed. He got us (and our luggage) in taxis headed for Sergei's. Sergei is the guy with Dad's conference who got us the hookup for places to stay in Moscow. My dad is all about seeing the "real" country when he goes somewhere, so it didn't surprise me that he'd requested we stay in people's homes.

We drove past about a gazillion identical apartment buildings until the taxis stopped at a tall one. Dad disappeared through the front door and came back with Sergei. Then he and Sergei took us to the different apartments where we'd stay the first two nights. Mom, Dad, and Lamont moved in with a family of four (up three flights of stairs). Joel and his dad stayed with an older man and his wife (only two flights up).

Mello and Harmony and I got to stay with a babushka and her little grandson. I loved them both immediately, even though they lived on the fourth floor. First chance to be flexible: no elevators, lots of luggage. At least the activity warmed us up.

The grandma looked just like a Russian babushka. I mean, I know that's what she was, but she was *so* perfect. If I looked up *babushka* in the dictionary, I might see a picture of her long hooked nose and pale blue eyes deep in a wrinkled face, with the scarf tied around her whole face. For reals.

Her grandson Alexi was maybe eight years old, with straight straw-blond hair and bright blue eyes. And he played the accordion for us. How cool is that?

Soon Sergei came to gather us all back into taxis, and we headed into Red Square. Mello fell asleep on the ride over, and I had to focus to keep my eyes open. We figured out it was the middle of the night back in California.

Ohwow, Red Square woke us up. It was bigger than I expected. I stood in the middle of the huge open part, turning slowly to see the elaborate GUM department store on one side and the pointy red wall in front of the yellow Kremlin (behind Lenin's mausoleum) on the other. And St. Basil's onion spires—each a different color, some striped, some zigzagged—made it look like a storybook castle come to life.

Mello kept saying, "We're really here. This is the real thing." And Harmony must have said "Cool frijoles" about four hundred times.

Lamont, of course, shot massive amounts of video.

We got some seriously crazy-fun pictures and bought loads of souvenirs. It took me ages to decide on a set of *matryoshka*—those famous nesting dolls that fit inside one another. I also found a way fabulous black jewelry box with flowers painted on it, and a gorgeous scarf.

Harmony scurried around, buying stuff for every member of her huge family.

Mello didn't buy anything, but she went back three times to look at a watch one of the street vendors had for sale.

I came up beside her. "Do you like it?" I asked.

She said, "Sort of."

I whispered, "Walk away again. He'll drop his price."

She shook her head. "He says he's offering me a good deal—but only for today."

I laughed and told her that was the classic line in every country: *Only for you, only today*.

She grinned at me, put the watch down, and took a few steps.

"Wait!" the man called. "All right, for you only, a very, *very* good deal."

I winked at her as she handed him the money and strapped her new watch onto her wrist.

•••

We had set a time to meet Lamont before dinner. I stood shivering at the meeting place with Mello and Harmony. Lamont was nowhere to be found.

"We should have had a buddy system. Why did we let him go off alone?" I asked. "I hate to lose him our very first day in Russia!"

"He's probably at that Internet café we passed," Harmony said, "checking email and seeing how many hits our site has gotten since we left."

"Maybe he's with Joel. There's Joel's dad," Mello said as we watched him join my parents.

Then two men walked by. They were so bundled up in their big coats and fur hats I couldn't see their faces. One said, "Your American friends are fine," in perfect English.

My jaw dropped. "That's creepy!" I said. "What's going on? Did someone kidnap Lamont and Joel?"

Mello rolled her eyes and said, "Come on, Trin. That *was* Lamont and Joel."

The "men" turned around and laughed. Yep. Tall, lanky Lamont and honey-blond Joel looked totally different in their puffy coats and traditional fur hats.

Sergei took us to a dinner-theater place where Russian dancers and singers in traditional costumes entertained us the whole time. Ohwow, they were amazing! Especially those men who cross their arms, squat, and kick. It hurt me to watch, so sometimes I looked across the table at Joel. Nothing painful about that.

One server placed trays of cold meats and vegetables on the table. Another brought each of us a bowl of borscht—a dark red beet soup.

"What's this white stuff floating on top?" I whispered to Mello.

"Probably the same stuff that was on the tomatoes and cucumbers," she whispered back. "It tastes like sour milk."

I decided to play it safe and stabbed a cold cut with my fork. I chewed forever, but it didn't go away. "This bologna stuff is really chewy," I mumbled to Harmony.

"Trin, that's not bologna," she answered. "It's cow's tongue. Didn't you see the taste buds along the edges?"

I looked in horror at the other pieces on the tray. She was right.

I spit the rubbery meat out of my mouth. It flew across the table and missed Joel's plate by a mere inch.

He and Harmony died laughing.

"The food is *different*, isn't it, Trin?" Harmony asked.

I glared at her. "At least I didn't shoot it out my nose like you would have," I answered, wiping my mouth and cleaning up the mess on the table.

One of the Russian men stepped to the microphone and said, "We understand we are not the only performers present tonight. Among our American friends we have visiting a band called the Chosen Girls."

We looked at each other and squealed. *How did they know?*

The man said, "We would like it very much if the Chosen Girls would sing for us."

I felt my face getting hot. Sing? Here? Now?

We didn't have our guitars or Mello's drums. We hadn't slept, really, for two days. I hadn't properly fixed my hair since the plane landed, and I still felt greasy and gross.

I leaned over to Mello and said, "This isn't how I pictured our Russian debut." And this definitely didn't match my hopes for the first time I'd perform in front of Joel.

Lamont smiled at me and said, "Be flexible."

I wanted to stick my tongue out at him, but the thought of *tongue* made me gag all over again.

I looked at Mello, expecting her to bail. Instead she stood up, grabbed my hand, and led me onto the stage. She smiled out at the audience, and they clapped even louder. Then she whispered, "Let's sing 'Love Lessons.' "

"We don't have our instruments," I whispered back.

She tried to talk without moving her lips. "I don't think they care. And I don't think we have a choice. It would be rude to say no. I'd start, but I can't because you sing lead." Her lips smiled, but her eyes focused on mine with a steely look. "Now sing!"

So I sang. Mello came in on harmony, and it actually sounded pretty decent. I couldn't decide if Harmony was lucky or unlucky not to come onstage. She just plays bass and doesn't sing.

Everyone clapped and cheered when we finished, and I wondered if they thought American rock bands always sang a cappella.

•••

When we got back to the apartment, I couldn't wait to take a bath and go to bed. I grabbed my PJs and headed for the bathroom. Our chubby little babushka met me in the dark hall and tried to explain how the hot water worked. At least I think that's what she explained.

She said something in Russian, and I said, "Huh?"

She said it again, a little louder. It didn't sound like anything on the Russian language CD. I held my hands up and shook my head to show I didn't understand.

She said it again, louder and slower. She was pretty much yelling. And she got right up next to me, looking up into my face.

I pulled out my English-Russian dictionary and tried to find whatever she kept repeating, but she flustered me so much I couldn't think. I turned pages, and she yelled. Not a mean yell, but the kind you might use to talk to someone hard of hearing.

I finally yelled back, in English. "Look, it doesn't matter how slowly you say it, or how loudly you say it, or how close to my face you are when you say it. I don't understand you!"

Mello giggled and said, "You're forgetting again, Trin. Go with the flow!"

That night we slept on the apartment's living room floor. Our babushka laid out a bunch of blankets, and really it made a pretty soft bed. When I finally got to lie down and close my eyes, I just wanted to sleep. But Mello and Harmony got a second wind and wanted to chat.

Mello said, "How cool was that, singing onstage in Russia?"

I didn't answer.

Harmony said, "You sounded great. And they loved it! This is going to be a seriously cool frijoles trip."

"Definitely," Mello agreed. "I'm so glad we came. It's even better than I imagined."

I just snuggled into my blanket and pretended to be asleep.

chapter • 6

•••

Two Days Later

On Monday night, we left Dad behind in Moscow and took a night train headed toward the border of Ukraine. Sweet. Each compartment had little shelves that pulled down and turned into beds. Okay, so they weren't at all comfortable, and the train stopped and started all night. But what rock band doesn't have a tough ride on their first tour?

The next day a bus ride took us far from the big city. On either side of the road, barren fields stretched as far as we could see. We passed people, bundled in their big hats and coats, walking down the lonely roads or driving horse-drawn wagons. It felt like we were riding backward through time.

Finally, the bus stopped in Clinsky, where we planned to spend the next five days. We gathered our stuff and got off the bus.

Nobody.

Anywhere.

"Where's our connection, Trin?" Harmony asked.

My heart flopped around inside me. "I'm sure he'll be here soon," I answered.

Harmony said, "Did you tell him what time to meet us?"

I rolled my eyes and said, "No, Harmony, I just hoped he would guess."

Mom said, "Trin, don't joke about that. We're in a foreign country, and it is a little scary if we don't make connections."

Lamont and Joel looked around. Lamont said, "I wonder if there's a phone somewhere. Do you have his number?"

I did not have his number. I had his address, though. I thought about trying to find a taxi, but just then an old white van pulled up. The passenger door flew open and a skinny guy ran up to us. "Verily, you are Chosen Girls, yes?" he said with a huge smile.

I smiled back and held out my hand. I said, "Yes. I'm Trin. Are you Pastor Kovitch?"

He shook my hand hard, then laughed until his curly black hair flopped over his eyes. "No, indeed. I say unto you, I am merely Sasha." He started loading our luggage through the back door of the van.

"I will be happily serving as your translator," Sasha said over his shoulder. "Here is Pastor Kovitch." He pointed to an older man coming around the van.

Pastor Kovitch's smile wasn't as big as Sasha's, but it was warm. He walked up to me, shook my hand, and pounded me on the back with his other hand as he said, "Welcome."

I smiled up at him and said, "Pastor Kovitch, thank you so much for hosting us. Ohwow, we are just way excited to be here! When's our first concert?"

He smiled and said, "Welcome."

I smiled bigger and whipped out my PDA, ready to type. "Thanks! I'm Trin, and I'm in charge of the Chosen Girls on this trip. I'd love to get a copy of our schedule so I can make plans. When's our first concert?" I said again, a little louder.

He smiled and turned away from me. He shook Mello's hand and said, "Welcome."

Lamont whispered, "I don't think he speaks English, Trin. Maybe talk a little slower?"

"Or even a little louder?" said Joel with a quick grin.

I ignored them. And Mello and Harmony, who were laughing their heads off.

Sasha spoke briefly with the pastor in Russian, then told us, "Verily, Pastor Kovitch says unto you that you are among welcome. He is pleased that thou hast joined him in ministry. On this day, and at this hour, we shall go to his home."

With that, Sasha picked up the last suitcases and headed for the van. Pastor Kovitch herded us into our seats.

"Great. So when is our first concert?" I asked their backs. I guess they didn't hear me. I put my PDA back in my bag.

We drove through the streets of Clinsky, lined with little cottages trimmed in bright colors. As we bumped over the dirt roads, Sasha talked cheerfully about every sight we passed.

"Cast your eyes unto our bakery," he said, pointing to the right. "And unto your left, ye shall see the dairy."

Lamont said, "You speak English well, Sasha."

He beamed and said, "Thank you. Indeed, I thank you. I taught myself to speak English, using the King James Bible!"

We dropped off Lamont and Joel, then continued down the block, where we dropped off Mom. Sasha pulled across the street to the front of Pastor Kovitch's home, trimmed in blue.

Mrs. Kovitch stood on the porch, tall and stout, with long brown hair. Like her husband, she had a warm smile. She asked us to take off our shoes as we came in the door. I happily obeyed.

Our stuff practically filled up their whole living room. Mrs. Kovitch led us straight to a table set for dinner.

A tray of bright red tomato slices and green cucumber slices sat in the middle of the table. I noticed the soured milk stuff was in a dish on the side. Sweet.

The pastor's wife walked back and forth from the kitchen, bringing more and more food. An adorable little boy trailed behind her, holding on to a piece of her skirt. She pointed to him and said, "Andrei." I waved and smiled at him. He hugged his mama tighter, but he did grin at me a little.

Finally, Mrs. Kovitch nodded to her husband. He stood and held out his hands. Sasha stood and took one. We all crowded around the table, standing and holding hands.

The pastor bowed his head and began to pray. I didn't understand most of what he said, but I did hear "Chosen Girls."

When we sat down, Mello said, "Isn't it excellent that God can understand every language?"

I smiled. "Yeah, it is."

I noticed two loaves of bread on the table. One was dark brown, almost black. The other looked like white bread.

Every meal we'd eaten so far in Russia included both the white and the black bread. I couldn't stand the black bread — it tasted like it had been baked with cough medicine or something.

I turned to Sasha and asked, "What do you call this brown bread?"

He said, "What?"

I repeated, "What do you call the brown bread?" I pointed to the loaf.

He just gave me a blank look.

I spoke more slowly. "You have white bread," I said, pointing to the white loaf. "You have brown bread," I said, pointing to the brown loaf. "Does the brown bread have a special name?"

He didn't answer. Harmony said, "He doesn't understand, Trin. Don't worry about it."

But now I was determined. This guy was our interpreter, after all. He had to understand us. I pulled off a piece of brown bread and held it up. "What do you call this?" I asked.

Sasha's eyes lit up and he nodded and smiled.

I sighed with relief. I had gotten through.

Sasha said, "Yes, you can take showers in the morning. Just do it!"

Mello and Harmony burst out laughing.

I tried my next question. "So when is our first concert?" I asked.

Sasha said something to the pastor, and the pastor said something back.

Sasha said, "Have you all had a pleasant journey?"

I smiled and said, "Ohwow, yes. We love Russia. And we're excited about doing concerts here. Are we going to do one tomorrow?"

Sasha spoke to the pastor again. The pastor smiled, nodded, and answered him. Then Sasha turned to me and said, "I say unto you, the pastor is so pleased that you enjoy our country. He understands you have brought medical supplies for the local hospital."

Mello said, "Yes, we each have a suitcase full. And toys for children."

“After supper you can put it all in boxes so it will be ready to give,” Sasha said.

“So we’re doing a concert at a hospital tomorrow?” I asked, trying to get back to the important stuff.

Sasha and the pastor chatted, then finally Sasha said with a smile, “Indeed, the doctors will be most pleased with your gift.”

“But what about concerts?” I asked.

Harmony said, “Come on, Trin, give up on it.”

“Oh, give up yourself,” I mumbled.

•••

Sasha left after dinner, and Mrs. Kovitch led us to a tiny building in the backyard.

“*Banya*,” she said and opened the door.

Steam poured out into the cold night. I stuck my head inside and saw a wooden bench on one side of the room and a kind of furnace on the other side. Mrs. Kovitch went in, picked up a ladle, and dipped water out of a big jug. Then she poured it over hot coals and more steam filled the room. She lit an oil lamp hanging on the wall.

She smiled and pointed to us, and then to a stack of towels on the bench.

“It’s a sauna!” Mello said.

“They have their own sauna? Cool frijoles!” Harmony added, stepping in. “Does that sound good or what?”

We squeezed inside, and Mrs. Kovitch smiled and nodded at us before she went out and closed the door.

We pulled off the clothes we’d traveled in and wrapped up in the towels. I squeezed my eyes shut and tried to let the heat seep all the way into my brain, but the questions just wouldn't steam away.

I so needed to know the plan. Why wouldn't they tell me about our first concert? Did Sasha and the pastor even understand my question? It seemed like they just didn't want to answer me.

Maybe there was a problem. Maybe the tour got called off, and nobody wanted to admit it. Or maybe the pastor didn't want to take responsibility for what we might do onstage.

"Trin, you no look-ah so good-ah," Mello crooned in a pathetic Russian accent. "It seems that the brown-ah bread of unknown-ah name, it no sit so good-ah in your belly."

I shut my eyes even tighter as Harmony's laughter filled the little room. "Was that supposed to sound Russian?" she asked.

I started grinning. I couldn't help it.

"Don't bother Trin," Harmony continued. "Look, she's dreaming about a certain cute guy we met on this trip. I can tell. And I don't blame her one bit."

Argh. My grin disappeared.

"And the lucky guy's name is ..." She leaned in and whispered, "Sasha!"

My eyes flew open in surprise.

Then we all died laughing.

•••

"Hey, the trip's been great," Harmony told me as we trudged back to the house. "Thanks for setting it up."

Another surprise. I smiled and said, "No problem."

And hoped she believed me.

chapter • 7

• • •

wednesday

"Doh-bray oo-tra, Trin."

My eyes adjusted, and I saw little Andrei smiling in my face. I smiled back, and he whispered it again. "Doh-bray oo-tra."

I whispered, "Good morning to you too, little guy." Mello and Harmony stirred under their blankets at the sound of Mrs. Kovitch's footsteps and then her voice. I couldn't understand her, but I had no doubt she said, "Get out of there right now. I told you not to wake them up!"

Andrei raised his eyebrows in an *uh-oh, I've-done-it-now* look and scampered away.

Sasha was already at the breakfast table, talking to the pastor, when we finished getting dressed.

"Verily, the pastor says unto you that you must get in the van."

I said, "Verily, are we doing a concert today?" Mello and Harmony hid their grins in their hands.

"He asks only that you get in the van," Sasha answered.

Harmony walked up. "Thank you, Sasha," she said sweetly. "Should we bring our equipment?"

Sasha spoke to the pastor again. Then he said, "Yes, please, you shall bring your equipment among you."

Mello turned to me. "Let the rocking of Russia begin!"

We changed into concert clothes, loaded the van, and picked up everyone else. Mom asked, "How are my girls?" as she climbed in. We told her about the banya. "I'll have to see if my hostess has one of those!" she said.

We drove over bumpy dirt roads, paved roads, and more dirt roads. I asked the name of the village we were heading to. Sasha talked to the pastor and then said, "Truly, it is a nearby village. We will be arriving there very soon."

I crossed my arms. What damage could come from me knowing the name of the village? Such a small thing.

We pulled up in front of an official-looking building. Pastor Kovitch spoke to Sasha, who said, "We shall unload your equipment here. Pastor Kovitch wants you shall do a concert."

Ohwow! My heart started pounding. Now that it was really here — our first concert in Russia — I felt a little crazy. "Let's go. This is it, Chosen Girls."

We hopped out of the van and started unloading equipment. We hauled stuff up the big cement steps of the building.

Pastor Kovitch tried the door.

Locked.

He said something to Sasha and took off walking around the building. I guess he hoped to find an open door. He didn't, because he came back and talked to Sasha again. Then he left.

Sasha said, "Indeed, he has gone to find the man with the key."

We sat on the steps. I watched my breath make little clouds in the cold air. Mello said, "What time does the concert start, Trin?"

"Like I know, Mello," I snapped. "Do you see them telling me anything?"

Pastor Kovitch came back alone. He said something to Sasha, who said something back in Russian. They went back and forth for a while, and neither of them sounded happy.

Finally, Sasha turned to us. "I say unto you, we are unable to unlock the building today. Indeed, you must perform your concert upon these very steps."

My frustrated huff made an extra-big cloud.

"Is there an electrical hookup?" Lamont asked.

Sasha gave him a blank look.

Lamont opened an amplifier case. He pulled out the end of a plug and pantomimed plugging it in.

Sasha nodded. "*Dah, dah*—yes. Plug. This you call plug, yes? For electric use."

Lamont sighed with relief. "Yes. You have a place we can plug in?" Again he acted out plugging in the cord.

Sasha's smile faded. "Verily I say unto you, inside this building there are many plugs. Here, though, on the steps—*nyet*. There are no plugs out here."

"So what do we have to do to get inside?" I asked. "We can't do a concert without electricity. I play electric guitar. Harmony's bass is electric. Even Mello's drums are electric! She borrowed them just for this tour because hers would take up, like, half the airplane."

Sasha stared at me. He didn't seem to get it. I walked up to the door and pulled on the handle myself, just in case.

Locked.

Beside the door, I noticed a large poster with Russian words written in red and blue ink. Sasha walked up beside me and pointed to it.

"You would like me to read this poster to you, indeed?" he asked.

I shrugged. "Does it say, 'The key is under the doormat'?"

Big-time blank look from Sasha. "No, this poster does not speak of the key. It speaks of the Chosen Girls," he answered.

Harmony said, "Cool frijoles! Read it, Sasha!"

Sasha smiled and did a little bow. "I shall. It says:

American Rock Stars

The Chosen Girls

All the way from California, America

Performing here!"

He pointed to the bottom, where someone had handwritten something. "This tells the time of today," he explained.

The words *American rock stars* got way stuck in my brain. Was the poster supposed to make me feel better or worse? We weren't going to sound much like rock stars without any juice running through our equipment.

"You see," Sasha said happily, "the people are coming!"

I didn't want to turn around, but I did. Men, women, young people, and kids gathered in at the bottom of the stairs.

"At least we know we're at the right place," I said. "And at the right time."

Harmony's eyes met mine. "Will you ever let me forget that?"

"Probably not," Lamont answered for me. "Let's figure out what you're going to do now, though."

"Right, Lamont," said Mello. "We have to fix this."

"You're our soundman," I told him. "You fix it!"

"I'm amazing, Trin," he answered. "But even I can't make your equipment work without electricity."

"We can't do anything, then. If only someone had told me where we were going, or when the concert was, I could have figured something out," I complained. "But no — everyone in Russia knew about today's concert but me and the man with the key. So we get dumped on some steps, the crowd comes, and I'm supposed to work a miracle."

"I think the miracle working is God's job," Mello said. "Why don't we pray for one right now?" She held her hands out to us.

I glanced back over my shoulder at the people standing in clumps at the bottom of the steps. Mom and Joel stood at the front of the crowd, looking worried.

I'm all for prayer, but it seemed a little late now. Still, what options did we have? I took one of Mello's hands and reached out to Harmony.

"Dear God," I prayed, "you know we want to honor you. We want to do a concert in this place that will help these people see your love. But our instruments and microphones won't work. What can we do? Please help us."

Mello prayed next. "God, this is an amazing opportunity. We're here in Russia, with people who have come to hear a concert. Help us be flexible. Help us honor *you*."

Harmony said, "We need you, God. Help us to know what to do."

"You are bigger than sound systems and instruments, God," Lamont prayed. "Let your love shine through these girls today. Amen."

When we looked up, Sasha stood there with a huge smile on his face, a guitar in one hand and a balalaika in the other. Pastor Kovitch stood behind him with a bongo drum or something.

They held them out to us.

So this was our answer to prayer?

Harmony took the guitar — of course. Mello took the bongo. That left me with the balalaika, a three-stringed, triangle-shaped Russian guitar.

I messed around with it, and a couple of people clapped. Ha!

I told Sasha, "Look, this isn't going to work. Make an announcement and explain what happened. Tell them to come back tomorrow — or whenever we can get inside and get plugged in."

Harmony played a few chords and adjusted the strings. "Shut your mouth and tune, Trin," she said.

I plucked the balalaika again and decided it sounded all right. As I worked out the fingering, I heard Pastor Kovitch's voice. He stood at the top of the steps, making an announcement.

Harmony whispered, "Sasha, what is he saying?"

"He says indeed we are unable to get into the building, thus you cannot plug in your equipment," he said.

I sighed with relief, glad he had decided to call it off.

The crowd clapped and cheered. Harmony, Mello, and I looked at each other. Harmony whispered, "Sasha, what is he saying now?"

Sasha translated, "He says that you are such talented performers that you will entertain them anyway. And at this time, he welcomes the Chosen Girls."

Mello looked at me and shrugged. Then she sat on a step and put that bongo drum between her knees. She said, "You've Chosen Me," and tapped out four beats. Harmony joined in, improvising on the guitar while Mello got a serious rhythm going on the drum. They sounded way fabulous. But I knew they couldn't do much without me, since I play lead guitar and sing the main part.

I was crazy-frustrated with the way this concert was going, but I did the only thing I could do. I hauled the balalaika to the middle of the "stage," and took charge. I sang my heart out and did the best I could on the new instrument, playing only the first two strings freestyle.

Mello started doing the echo part, and something weird happened. Standing outside, with just our voices and the acoustic instruments, "You've Chosen Me" sounded like a whole different song. It seemed almost Russian.

I could tell the people felt it too. They really cheered for us. We even did our Lord's Prayer song in their language. The words had to be close to right, because, ohwow, it was a huge hit.

In between songs, I explained their meaning, and Sasha translated for us. I hoped he got it right without telling them to go home and bathe or anything.

During the fourth song, I noticed the crowd shifting and moving around. I thought, *Oh, no! We're losing them. They're getting bored.* But that wasn't it at all. I heard a loud *moo*, and in came the cows. For real—a small herd of cattle plodding right through the middle of our audience. The babushka herding them along looked up and waved at us as she shooed them past.

I wanted to laugh or cry, but since I couldn't decide which, I just kept singing. We finally made it to the last song.

After the concert, Pastor Kovitch stood up to speak, and Sasha led us to a row of boxes. "Verily I say unto you, the pastor asks that you give these out."

"What are they?" Joel asked, joining us.

"These are Bibles. Many people in this village do not own a Bible," he explained.

We took our places behind the boxes, and as soon as the pastor said, "Amen," the people started pushing and shoving to get the Bibles. We handed them out as quickly as we could—even Mom came and helped.

"Why are they so pushy?" Mello asked.

"Their country has been through some tough times," Lamont answered. "Lots of times, these people have probably waited for something that was gone before they ever got to the front of the line."

"And not having a Bible ...," Harmony added. "Can you imagine? I think I have three. I don't even know how many are in my house."

I smiled at a little girl as I handed her a Bible. I wanted to tell her what a difference it could make. I wanted her to know God loved her—that he had chosen her. But she left and an older man stood in her place. I handed him one too, and then gave one to a woman my mom's age. I thought about the awesome privilege of giving people the very words of God, and I almost started crying.

When everyone had a Bible, Sasha led us down the street to a house. Inside, a group of older ladies stood smiling at us from behind a table piled with food.

"Ohwow! That looks so good!" I said to them. I didn't even care that they couldn't understand me. "I didn't know how hungry I was!"

They smiled even bigger, and I thought maybe they could understand — at least my smile.

We sat down to a lunch of more tomatoes and cucumbers and potatoes and bread.

I tried to scrape the Russian sour cream off a cucumber with a fork. "So how weird is it that they put sour cream on everything but the potato?" I whispered.

"And watch out for the gelatin," Lamont said. "It's not really Jell-O. I think it's congealed chicken broth."

"Chicken Jell-O!" I answered. "Ew. Where's a good old McDonald's when you need one? How do people eat this every day?"

Lamont said, "Maybe we could suggest chicken Jell-O to Mr. Walling. It could be a new side dish at Chik'n Quik."

We didn't laugh.

"Hey, uh, good job today, women," he said, changing the subject. "But didn't you feel like that concert got a little long?"

I snapped my head up. "No. We sang the same number of songs we always do. Why?"

He tore off a piece of white bread and handed the loaf to Joel.

"That's for sure, Lamont," Joel said. "At one point I thought, 'They're going to sing until the cows come home!' "

I flipped my hair at their obvious setup, while they cracked up. Mello turned to Harmony and explained. "That's an American saying from when everyone farmed. It means somebody just won't quit till the end of the day, when the cows come home."

Harmony said, "I know that, Mello. Just because I'm from another country doesn't mean I'm stupid."

Mello's eyes got all teary. "I'm sorry, Harmony," she said. "I don't think you're stupid."

Harmony looked at me. "Trin, you said we should remember things in a new country are different—not weird."

I blinked. Where did this come from? "Yeah, I said that."

"But you are totally making fun of the food," she said. "You have no idea what kind of sacrifices these people have made so we can eat like this."

I looked down at my plate. "Ohwow, Harmony, you're right. I've been way rude."

"Sī, you have," Harmony said. "Since we first talked about this trip, you've been Miss Foreign Relations. But guess what? I am *from* a foreign country, and yeah, things are different. People don't have money here. They're giving up food from their own tables to feed us. Show some respect."

I felt like crawling under the table. Even Lamont clenched his teeth. But Harmony wasn't finished.

"You prayed for people to see our love and they did," she said. "Maybe you ought to think about seeing their love too."

Nobody spoke another word till Sasha came to load us all back into the van, but I ate every bite of the chicken Jell-O.

chapter • 8

• • •

Still Wednesday

We drove along for a while before Sasha said, "You have heard of Chernobyl?"

"That's where the nuclear power plant blew up, right?" Lamont asked. "Wasn't that back in the 1980s?"

"Dah, 1986. It was a terrible thing for our country," Sasha answered. "Many people had to run to save their lives."

Joel asked, "Is there still radiation around?"

Sasha nodded. "Indeed, there is a place near Chernobyl that is still called the dead zone."

I felt a shiver run up my spine.

"In the dead zone, radiation is so strong that some say no one may live there for at least another six hundred years," Sasha explained. "Maybe nine hundred. The houses, schools, and businesses are still there. But they are all empty."

"Like ghost towns," Harmony said in an awed whisper.

I looked out the front of the van and noticed some kind of warning sign blocking the road. Pastor Kovitch pulled the van over and parked.

"We have arrived," Sasha said. "You may get out now."

I didn't see a concert hall or any people. "Where are we?" I asked.

Sasha looked surprised. "Why, we are at the dead zone," he answered.

"I don't get it. Are we here on purpose?" Mello asked as we climbed out of the van.

"I think this is Sasha's idea of a cool tourist site," Lamont said.

Ahead, we saw houses and other buildings. Sasha climbed over the barrier and walked toward them. We followed him.

"That must have been a school," Mello said, pointing to a rectangular brick building with a swing set beside it. The wind blew the swings back and forth. I imagined the children who used to swing there, and I shivered again.

Harmony pointed to a different building with a large sign on the front. "I bet that was a store."

"Dah," Sasha said. "The sign says Bicycles for Sale."

"It feels weird to be in the middle of a town like this and not hear cars and people," Joel commented. "It's so quiet."

"It's too quiet," Harmony agreed. "Sasha, is it okay for us to be here? I mean, the people had to leave because of the radiation, right? Is this safe?"

Sasha nodded gravely. "You be here for one hour, you run, you jump, you laugh. But if you remain here for one day ..." He looked around before turning back to us to say, "You must be dead."

"Well, I've seen enough!" Lamont said abruptly. He turned back to the van.

We followed him quickly.

"That was weird," Mello said as we got in and found our seats.

Lamont said, "I think the Chosen Girls should have a new motto after this."

"What?" Harmony asked.

He smiled. "The Chosen Girls: Radiating God's Love."

I rolled my eyes.

"I've got another one," Harmony said. "The Chosen Girls: Glowing for Jesus."

As we drove back to the pastor's home, I realized he didn't live far from the dead zone. With Sasha's help, I asked Pastor Kovitch about it before dinner. "Is there a lot of radiation around here too?"

Sasha listened to the pastor's answer then told me, "Yes, it is higher than normal here. That is why we have plenty of food to eat. People in the rest of Russia don't want to eat food that we grow here, near Chernobyl."

"But aren't you worried about it?" I asked.

Pastor Kovitch shook his head. Sasha translated. "Not so much for me." Then tears started running down the pastor's face. He pointed to his little boy, who sat on the floor stacking up blocks, and Sasha translated, "It is my son who will suffer, because he is growing up with the radiation. And it is very possible that his children will have deformities or diseases because of it."

I couldn't imagine. "Why do you stay here? Why don't you move?"

The pastor smiled at me and said through Sasha, "The people here need a pastor. Many of them can't move away—this is where their homes and families are. They need someone to teach them about God."

I felt tears running down my own face as my heart filled with a new love for this man who was so devoted to God's call.

•••

That night, Lamont and Joel came over to hang with Mello, Harmony, and me.

"It's harder than I thought—being in another country," Mello said.

Harmony nodded. "Sī, it's frustrating not being able to talk to people. How can we make a difference if they can't even understand us?"

"You should have listened to your language CDs," I reminded her. "I told you over and over before we left the States, but you wouldn't believe me. Now you see how important it is."

She said, "Oh, whatever. I don't hear you chatting it up in Russian, Trin."

Joel said, "No way could a beginner explain the gospel in Russian, Trin. Think about it."

"That's right," Lamont agreed. "No matter how many times we listened to your CDs. What we need is a way to communicate without words. Like a pantomime."

Harmony almost jumped off the couch. "Cool frijoles! Lamont, you're a genius."

"Definitely. What an excellent idea," Mello agreed.

"You mean like mimes with white gunk on their faces?" I asked, holding up my hands and pretending to touch the walls of an invisible box closing in around me. "How can we help anybody by pretending to be in a box?"

"You can act out any kind of story, Trin—try thinking *outside* the box," Lamont answered.

"Yeah," Harmony said, "like, try thinking something might be a good idea even if you aren't the person who thought of it."

"Ohwow! That was rude," I said. "I do not think I'm the only person with good ideas."

"Tell me one time you liked an idea you didn't think of," Harmony insisted.

"Well," I said. "Just give me a second."

"Exactly!" she said.

"This isn't helping," Joel said. "What could you do a pantomime about?"

"Did you bring your superhero suits?" Lamont asked.

"Sí," Harmony answered.

"And your swords and shields?"

Mello said, "Uh-huh."

"How about a skit about the power of prayer?" Lamont suggested.

Mello nodded. "Excellent. Maybe we could kind of act out the scenes from the "You've Chosen Me" video, where each of us is being attacked by P. Ride, Jealous E, and Rival Ree."

I glared at Lamont and said, "It's a toss-up on who should play the part of the demons, but I have a couple of ideas."

•••

Thursday

I didn't want to admit it, but the skit turned out way cool. The next day we went to an orphanage — the perfect place to try it out.

"It's a good thing I reminded everyone to bring the white suits so we'd have the stuff for the skit," I told Harmony. "There must be a hundred little kids here."

She said, "Sí. We got lucky this time. You really should try to find out where we're going each day, Trin, so we can be prepared."

I growled and went to get my guitar.

We set up on a makeshift stage and performed an all-out concert for the kids, who clapped harder than any of our other audiences. Sometimes I had to sing looking up at the ceiling because I wanted to cry looking at those beautiful faces. I wished I could take them all home, so they could grow up in a family.

About halfway through, we sang "You've Chosen Me." Then Sasha came up onstage to explain what the song meant. When he stepped down, we started the skit. Harmony and I acted out a fight. It wasn't too hard to pretend on that part. Then Lamont came slithering toward Mello in a red costume we had thrown together. The kids squealed and shrieked and tried to warn her, but he attacked with his laser eyes. No real lasers, just Lamont pointing his fingers. Mello went crazy — stomping and snorting around, sticking her nose in the air and making fun of me. She did a great job exaggerating what jealousy looks like. I couldn't believe shy Mello could turn it on like that. The kids loved it.

Next, Harmony came onstage and she and I had it out. Then Lamont got her. Harmony made Mello's craziness look totally calm. She acted out rivalry, running over to me and pointing back at Mello, then going to Mello and pretending to whisper things about me. The kids giggled, and I knew they understood what she was doing. No doubt kids everywhere — even Russia — act that way.

Lamont got me last. I acted out pride. I stuck my nose in the air and looked down at the other two, and walked around them shaking my finger at them. I pointed to myself to show them they needed to be more like me.

We turned away from each other and stomped off to separate parts of the stage. Then, one at a time, we let our shoulders droop and made sad faces to show we didn't like the way we were acting.

Mello dropped to her knees in prayer, Harmony walked over and knelt beside her, and I came and knelt beside Harmony. Lamont switched off the spotlight long enough for us to quickly peel away our normal concert clothes to reveal our superhero suits underneath.

We leaped up, dressed in white from head to toe, as Lamont flipped on the strobe lights. We grabbed our swords and shields and stood poised for battle.

Lamont tried to creep up to Harmony. She did a karate roundhouse kick and pointed her sword at him. She held it like it had so much power coming out of it she could hardly stand up, and Lamont shook like he was being electrocuted. He fell back and the kids cheered madly.

He lay there for a while, shaking and kicking. Then he started slithering toward Mello. She raised her sword and pretended to jab at him. He started shaking again, and did a slow-death scene worthy of an Academy Award. The children went way crazy.

When he raised his head again, he looked at me, then at the kids, then back at me, like, "Should I try it?" The kids shouted, "Nyet! Nyet!"

He didn't take their advice. He took a few huge breaths and dragged himself to me on his elbows. I had no mercy. I twirled around and then brought my sword down, pointed at his back. This time he shook and twitched for ages. He slowed down, until he finally stopped and lay still. When the kids began to cheer, he did one last twitch.

Harmony and Mello and I sheathed our swords and grabbed each other's hands. We each put a foot on Lamont's back to symbolize our triumph, and we raised our hands and eyes to God in praise.

The children stood up and clapped and yelled. It was way fabulous.

We finished out the concert in our superhero suits. Afterward, we gave away the toys. The kids loved them. I guess they don't have as many toys as most kids in the States. We also signed autographs for the kids and took pictures with them. I figured if I couldn't take the kids home, at least I could take their pictures with me. And as I looked into their eyes and drank in their smiles, I knew they would always have a place in my heart.

I asked Sasha if we were going to go to any more orphanages. He said, "Indeed, I do not believe we will today." And when I asked where we were going next, he just walked away.

Back in the van, Harmony said, "I love those kids! I want them all!"

"Me too," Mello agreed.

"What's next, Trin?" Lamont asked. "Do we have another concert today?"

I couldn't tell if he was serious or if he just wanted to torture me into admitting I didn't have a clue.

chapter • 9

•••

Still Thursday

The van pulled up in front of a tall building, and I dashed to get to Sasha the moment he got out.

"Are we doing a concert here?"

"Nyet," he answered.

"What are we doing, then?" I asked, determined to get a handle on this thing, language barrier or not.

"Verily, you are going to give the supplies you brought," he answered.

I looked up at the building. "Is this a hospital?"

"Indeed, it is."

Sweet! I had information. I opened the door of the van and stuck my head in.

"OK, everybody, listen up," I said. "This is a hospital, and we're going to take in the medical supplies we brought."

"Are we doing a concert?" Mello asked.

A question I could answer! "No concert," I said with a smile.

"But we're dressed in our superhero suits," Harmony pointed out.

Why hadn't I realized that?

"I'm not going into a hospital dressed like this," Mello complained.

I looked down at my white outfit. "Of course not. We're going to put our other clothes back on over these." I climbed in and grabbed my clothes. We grunted and groaned as we struggled to get our stuff on in the crowded van.

Finally dressed, we got out. Lamont and Sasha had already lined up the boxes of supplies on the sidewalk.

I said, "Each of you grab a box." We followed Pastor Kovitch inside. He shook hands with some important-looking people, and soon we were surrounded by doctors and nurses who talked loudly and looked through the boxes we held.

One nurse picked up a bottle of aspirin and held it high, calling out words in Russian. Everyone murmured happily. They reminded me of little kids at Christmas.

A doctor finally took my box from me. He looked at me with tears running down his face and said, "Spah-see-bah!"

I swallowed a lump in my throat and said, "You're welcome." I couldn't even remember how to say it in Russian. I felt overwhelmed. I couldn't imagine what it would be like to run a hospital without basic stuff like aspirin.

I remembered that I hadn't liked the idea of bringing medical supplies—or toys—when Harmony and Mello suggested it. I hadn't wanted to mess with it. Now I just wished I had brought more.

One of the important-looking men called for everyone's attention. He spoke in a loud voice. When he finished, everyone looked at us and cheered.

Sasha explained, "He said you are a group called Chosen Girls, rock stars from America, traveling in Russia doing concerts. He said you thought of us before you ever left your country and gathered up these supplies for our hospital. He said you are more than rock stars. You are heroes!"

I looked down, embarrassed. I could see the legs of my superhero suit sticking out below my cropped pants. If they could see my cruddy attitude, they'd know why I didn't much feel like a hero.

We went back to our village. After we changed clothes, Mrs. Kovitch signaled that the three of us should follow her. She took little Andrei by the hand and walked out the door.

Harmony said, "Where are we going, Trin?"

"Why are you asking me?" I snapped, walking out behind the pastor's wife. "Why does everyone always ask me?"

Mello followed and said, "Because you act like you know everything."

I rolled my eyes. "Whatever."

"Whatever?" Mello echoed. "You want so bad to be in charge. You've been in charge of everything your whole life, haven't you? You took control of Harmony and me the week you moved to California."

I said, "What? I took control of you?"

"Who started the band? Who entered us in the contest?"

"So I suggested we might enter a contest, and you think—"

Mello stomped along behind Mrs. Kovitch and Andrei. "Suggested. Right. Just like you *suggested* coming to Russia."

"Are you saying you wish we didn't have a band?" I asked.

"That's not what I'm saying," Mello answered.

"So you wish we hadn't come to Russia?" I continued.

Mello shook her head. "I love it here. I'm definitely glad we came."

I stopped walking and put my hands on my hips. "I don't get you, Mello. If you're glad about Chosen Girls and you're glad about the trip, what are you griping about?"

Mello ignored me and turned to Harmony. "If you take away the control freak's control, what do you have?"

Harmony said, "Come on, Mello. Quit."

"Just a freak!" Mello said, answering her own riddle and whirling toward me. "Am I right, Trin? You can't stand it here because it's the first time in your life you aren't in control."

"You're just jealous," I snapped back. "You're always in the background. You say you like it there. But really, I think you want to be like me. You wish you could get things done. Well, I'm sorry, but I'm not letting you—or Pastor Kovitch—ruin this trip."

I turned away from her and followed Mrs. Kovitch down the street again. "Talk about a person who thinks she knows everything," I muttered. Mrs. Kovitch and her son went inside a little shop and we went in after them.

Harmony pointed to a large photograph on the wall—a picture of an ice-cream sundae. "Look, Mello! Look, Trin!" she said happily. "This is an ice-cream shop. No fighting in here, *amigas*. Just ice cream and happy times, OK?"

I sat in silence and watched little Andrei eat his ice cream. He got a drop of it on the end of his nose, and he giggled and giggled. I laughed too. But then I started thinking about him growing up with all that radiation, and my eyes got teary. Then I thought at least he had a family—not like the kids at the orphanage.

I couldn't stop the tears. They just kept running down my face. I used my napkin and tried to turn away so no one would see me.

Mrs. Kovitch looked worried. I'm sure she wondered what my deal was—she takes me out for ice cream and I cry the whole time.

Mello thought it was her fault. "I'm sorry, Trin," she said. "I should have kept my mouth shut about the control thing."

"It's not that," I said. "He got ice cream on his nose and it made me think about radiation and that made me think about the orphans and—" I stopped long enough to start sobbing. "It's all just ... so ... sad!" I put my arms on the table and buried my head in them. I could feel Harmony and Mello patting my shaking shoulders. I felt like an idiot. An absolute, double-scoop, deluxe idiot.

Then I felt little Andrei's arms reaching around my neck. I turned and gathered him up, and held him while I cried. He used his chubby little fingers to wipe the tears off my face, which of course made me cry all over again.

By the time I pulled myself together, my ice cream had melted. I scooped up the strawberry-flavored milk with my spoon and slurped it. Then I managed a weak smile and a *spah-see-ba* for Mrs. Kovitch.

Harmony echoed my thanks, and I didn't even care that Mello wouldn't meet my eyes.

chapter • 10

•••

Friday

The next day we drove up in front of a huge brick auditorium with people filing inside.

"Look! The doors are open!" Harmony said. "We'll be able to plug in!"

Mello looked terrified. "So many people! I bet that place could hold thousands."

I whipped out a compact and checked my hair in the little mirror. "OK, this is going to be the concert we were meant to give," I said. I handed the mirror to Harmony. "I'm in charge and nothing is going to go wrong. You primp while I go over the details. Same format as the orphanage. We'll do the skit after 'You've Chosen Me.' I'm way glad we'll have juice this time." I turned to Lamont. "You're sure the electrical converters are good to go?"

"No problem," he answered. "We have some of the biggest ones they make."

"Mello, you don't have the blue hair stuff in the van, do you?"

"No," she said. "But I just sprayed it this morning."

"I think it could use more," I told her. "You feeling okay about the electric drum set?"

"Definitely. I'm getting used to it. But I did like that bongo the other day," she answered. "It felt very back-to-nature to beat something with my hands."

Lamont said, "OK, Nature Woman, remind me to never put a real drum in your hands again."

"Harmony, don't forget we switched the Russian song to *G*."

"Sī," Harmony answered. "Cool frijoles! I'm ready to rock."

I opened the van door. "Everybody is responsible for their own equipment," I reminded them. "It looks like we could be on any time now. Grab your stuff and let's go!"

I ran around and opened the back of the van. I reached for my guitar, but Sasha said, "Nyet. You shall not be needing to carry your equipment."

"It's okay, Sasha, we're used to it," I explained. "Besides, Joel and Lamont will help. This is a performance, right?"

"Nyet. Well, dah," he said. "Verily, I say unto you, it is a performance, but—"

I rolled my eyes. "We don't have time to verily right now, Sasha. I'm trying to run this band, and you aren't helping me any. We're obviously late for this concert, so we've got to hurry! Harmony, grab your guitar and an amp. Mello, grab your drums and an amp. Lamont and Joel, get everything else."

I took my stuff and started running for the building. I could hear the others coming behind me.

People walking into the building stopped to stare at us. I figured it must be way obvious we were the American band they were coming to see. Between my pink hair, Mello's blue hair, and our wildest clothes, we for sure didn't blend into the crowd.

All the Russians wore browns or blacks and totally subdued styles. We even passed a group of girls in black dresses. Lamont said, "They sure get dressed up for rock concerts over here."

I called over my shoulder, "I guess it's a big deal. I wish we had time to sign autographs!"

Harmony said, "We'll have time afterward. Let's get set up."

We headed into the building and straight down the aisles, past hundreds of people who were already seated.

"Gorgeous auditorium," Mello huffed as we jogged up the steps and onto the stage.

"I'm not really in the mood to appreciate the architecture," I snapped. "I hate this. Why couldn't they get us here in time to set up?"

"Nothing like tuning up in front of hundreds of people," Harmony agreed.

Lamont helped me plug in my amp and guitar with the converters. Joel, of course, helped Harmony. I strummed a chord and smiled as the sound filled the building. It would be great to finally do a real concert in a real concert hall.

I looked around while I tuned. I noticed Pastor Kovitch in a heated discussion with a man in a suit. The man pointed to us and said something. He didn't look at all happy.

I said, "Look, the pastor is getting in trouble for bringing us so late. But we're going to be so awesome that everyone forgets about it. Got it?"

"Definitely," Mello agreed as she warmed up on her drums with a roll on the snare and a few cymbal crashes.

Harmony played a bass pattern and said, "There's Sasha."

Sasha joined the discussion with Pastor Kovitch. Then he headed toward us, practically running.

"Lamont, Joel, get off the stage," I said. "It looks like Sasha is coming to introduce us."

Lamont smiled. "We finished just in time," he said.

Sasha dashed up the steps.

I flashed him my biggest smile. "Bet you never saw a band set up this fast, did you? We're ready."

His face turned red. He nodded, took a big breath, and nodded again. "Verily, I say unto you, you set up very fast, but—"

"So introduce us," I said. "We're ready to rock, and those people out there look like they're ready for a concert."

"They are ready," Sasha said, stopping to lick his lips, "for a choral youth competition."

"A choir contest?" Harmony asked. "We're a rock band. What are we doing at a choir contest?"

"Unfortunately," Sasha answered, "I am utterly unable to answer that question. I tried to tell you not to bring your equipment, but you did not listen unto me." He drilled little holes into my eyeballs.

"You mean, the Chosen Girls aren't performing here?" Mello asked. That familiar look of panic and embarrassment covered her face.

Sasha smiled and nodded, obviously relieved. "Indeed! The Chosen Girls are part of the audience today." He pointed to the hundreds—maybe thousands—of people in the auditorium. "The Chosen Girls shall sit and enjoy the Russian choirs." He looked at the man in the suit, who now waited, arms crossed, in the wings. A group of about twenty Russian young people stood behind him — the girls in long black dresses, the boys in white dress shirts and black pants. "You shall remove your equipment now, yes?" Sasha finished.

I wanted to run backstage and hide, or take the next plane home to America. But instead we quickly, quietly cleared the stage and took our seats.

I scrunched down in my seat beside Mom as the first performers filed onto the stage.

"Don't they look cultured, standing straight and tall in those long black dresses? They are so classy," Mom whispered. I looked down at my pink lace-up shirt and cropped pants, and tucked my high-heeled boots under my seat.

"Aren't they amazing?" Mom said while we clapped for the fourth choir. "That's true talent! They must study classical music for years to sing like that."

She might as well have said, *Not like your band, Trin, that just gets together in some garage shed and makes stuff up.*

The sad song the next choir sang matched my mood. My big attempt to run the band went way beyond disaster, and Mom picked the worst possible place to tell me I'm not truly talented or classy.

"Why do all their songs sound sad?" Mello whispered. "Everything is in a minor key."

"I don't know," I whispered back. "Maybe because life stunk here for so long. Or maybe they're sad for us, since we just embarrassed ourselves so completely."

While the man in the suit announced the winners, Lamont leaned over. "Maybe the Chosen Girls will win for shortest performance. Are you still sticking around to sign autographs?" he asked.

I stuck my tongue out at him.

•••

Pastor Kovitch's church choir won the whole thing. He came around, beaming and shaking hands. He looked so happy I guess he forgave us for almost bombing the entire competition. And the choir members kept coming up, shaking our hands and trying to talk to us. You'd have thought we really did do a concert instead of just humiliating ourselves.

We finally got out our Russian-English dictionaries and attempted some conversations. Of course, Sasha got in the mix too. I mostly talked to Natalia, a tall girl with long blonde hair. She said she loved my hair and my clothes, so I felt a little better. I told her congrats on winning the contest, and she smiled a huge smile.

I saw Mom watching Natalia and me. I wondered if she wished she could switch us out—leave me in Russia and take quiet, classy, award-winning Natalia home.

I decided I wouldn't blame her if she did.

chapter • 11

• • •

Still Friday

I couldn't decide who I was most mad at—myself for rushing onto a stage we didn't belong on, the pastor for not revealing one plan ever, or Sasha for just verily getting "unto" my last nerve. Mello and Harmony obviously didn't feel my pain.

"You're amazing, Trin," Harmony began as soon as we got back to the pastor's house. "I didn't *think* I could ever be more embarrassed than the day I took us to the wrong park, and then I *knew* I'd never be more embarrassed than when we did a concert in chicken suits. But you managed to show me up."

"You got that right," Mello agreed. "Setting up for a concert in front of a thousand people waiting for a classical music competition!" She looked in the hall mirror and added, "And I'm dressed like this! And my hair is blue!"

"Would you get over your blue hair?" I sputtered.

Harmony crossed her arms. "It was bad, Trin. Seriously. I mean, I know I don't have much room to talk. I've made my share of mistakes. But, wow! That was a big one."

I sat down and started unlacing my boots. "Raise your hand if you think it must be fun to be you," I said. "Just along for the ride, enjoying the countryside. You don't have the pressure of coordinating this trip, Harmony. You either, Mello. All you two have to do is go where you're told. So why don't you get off my back? I'm doing the best I can."

"In what way?" Mello asked, sitting on the floor to pull off her own boots. "Not to be rude, but how exactly are you coordinating this trip? You don't have a clue what we're doing."

"Sí," Harmony agreed. "I don't think you know any more than we do."

I jumped up off the couch. "Ohwow. That's it." I stomped out of the room.

"Where are you going?" Harmony called.

I looked back at her. "To find the pastor."

Pastor Kovitch sat at the table in the kitchen, reading a newspaper.

I said, "Excuse me. May I speak to you, please?"

He looked up and smiled. He said, "Welcome."

I groaned. How could I find out what I needed to know? I pulled my little English-Russian dictionary out of my pocket. I tried to find *plan*. I couldn't find it. I did find *I learn*, so I said that: "Ee-zoo-chah-yoo." Then I flipped the pages until I found *tomorrow*: "zhav-tra." That was as close as I could get to saying, "I want to learn what we're doing tomorrow."

He smiled and said, "Hah-ra-shoh."

That means *good*.

Maybe he thought I meant I would learn something tomorrow. Like not to run up onto the stage when I wasn't supposed to.

Argh!

I looked around the kitchen. Mrs. Kovitch stood at the sink peeling potatoes, with little Andrei at her feet. I asked, "Sasha?"

The pastor spilled out a stream of Russian. At the end of it he pointed to me and said, "*Mhat.* Mama?"

I said, "Is Sasha at the house my mom's staying at? Is that what you're saying? Can I go get him so he can translate?"

The pastor smiled and shook his head. He said something to his wife and she turned around and shrugged. I tried again. I pointed to myself and said, "Mhat." Then I pointed in the direction of the house she was in. "Sasha." And I pointed toward that house again.

"Dah!" the pastor and his wife both said. "Dah, dah!"

I smiled and said, "I'll go get him. I'll be right back."

I ran down the street and found the right house. I knocked on the door and asked for Sasha. I couldn't believe how relieved I felt to see him. "Sasha, can you come translate, please? I'm trying to speak to the pastor," I explained.

"Indeed!" he answered. "I say unto you, I will be pleased to help you on this day."

•••

Back in the Kovitch kitchen I whipped out my PDA, flipped it on, and said, "I want to know what we are doing tomorrow, please."

Sasha looked like the question hurt him. He spoke to the pastor, who also didn't look excited about it. After the pastor answered, Sasha said, "Verily, I say unto you, tomorrow should be a good day for you and your friends."

I clenched my fists and took a deep breath before I said, "Sasha, that's not what I want to hear and you know it. Tell me exactly what we are doing tomorrow. I want the names of the villages we're going to and the times we'll be at each one. And I want to know if we're doing concerts or greeting orphans or listening to Russian choirs. Now!"

Sasha didn't even repeat my questions to the pastor. He said, "Indeed, the pastor will not answer these questions."

I felt tears running down my face. "But why not? Why is everything a secret? Why can't he tell me what's going on? Ohwow, it's making me crazy!"

The pastor said something to Sasha, and they started a whole big conversation in Russian. Mrs. Kovitch got into it too. I think maybe she felt sorry for me. I hoped she would tell her husband to give it up and let me in on the details.

Finally, Sasha turned back to me. "Verily I say unto you, the Americans are sometimes different from the Russians, dah?"

"Well, now, there's something we can agree on, Sasha," I said.

"In your country, it is important to be on time I think, and to have a plan," he continued.

I nodded. "Of course," I agreed.

Sasha nodded. "Pastor Kovitch has plans, yes, but the Lord may change those plans, dah?" he explained. "In Russia, many, *many* times things do not go as we plan them to. We do not like to disappoint our guests from America if these plans must change. So Pastor asks, please, that you trust him. He has made good plans for you. You trust him, and he will trust the Lord, dah?"

I sank down onto a kitchen chair. So that was it. I was defeated.

Sasha patted my shoulder. "I think it is very difficult for you to trust others, dah? Perhaps you like very much to be in control of things?"

I put my face in my hands and mumbled, "Dah."

After supper, Mrs. Kovitch led us back out to the banya. When we were all wrapped in our towels and the steamy mist, I told Mello and Harmony the bad news.

"I'm sorry. I'm a failure. I absolutely demanded Pastor Kovitch tell me tomorrow's plans, but he wouldn't." I wiped a washcloth across my sweaty face. "You're both right. I don't have clue one about what we're doing."

Harmony gave my shoulder a squeeze. "That doesn't make you a failure, Trin," she said.

I looked at her in surprise. "Of course it does. Raise your hand if you think a leader needs to know what's going on in order to lead."

Mello shook her head and said, "Sometimes a leader just needs to know who to follow. Maybe on this trip, we should just trust Pastor Kovitch to show us what to do."

"That's exactly what he said," I told her. "That he wants us to trust him, as he trusts the Lord."

"Is that so bad?" Harmony asked.

"Yes, it is! I don't know what we're doing tomorrow!" I shouted.

Harmony said, "OK, Trin, what if I told you I had the scoop?"

"No way."

"Just listen," she continued. "We're going to Dharstvenyee at 9:00 a.m. to do a concert in a concert hall. At noon, we'll do another concert in Kahkboda, and the people there will serve us lunch afterward. Then at 3:00 p.m. we'll do one last concert at a church in Skhabyanoy. Do you feel better now?"

"Ohwow, yes. But how did you find all that out? Did you listen to Pastor and Sasha through the wall or something?" I asked.

"Wait," Harmony continued. "Now tell me how to get to that first village—the one that starts with a *d*."

I laughed at her. "Yeah, right."

"OK," she said, "how about the other two? Do you know where they are?"

"No. Do you?" I asked.

"Nope," she answered. "So how does knowing the plan really help us? If the van broke down or the pastor got sick, it's not like we'd know how to get there."

"Your point is?" I asked.

"I get it," Mello interrupted. "Even if you know the plan, you aren't in control, Trin. None of us are. Not even when it's stored in a PDA. We just don't know enough to take charge. That's why the pastor is asking us to trust him."

"But it's so hard!" I complained. "I'd rather do it myself."

"Remember what happened when you did?" Harmony reminded me. "Disaster at the choir contest."

"Do you see what this is?" Mello asked. "This is a total life lesson, happening right here in the Russian banya."

Harmony made a face at her and said, "What?"

"This isn't just about control during the Russia trip. This is about who will control our whole lives. Get it? We're just as clueless bumbling through life as we are about getting around in Russia," she said. "Over here, the pastor knows the language and the places, and we can trust him to make the plans for us."

"I get it!" Harmony blurted out. "In life, God is the one who has it all figured out. We can run around trying to be in charge—"

"And make stupid mistakes," I added.

"Or we can trust God with the plans," Harmony finished.

"Ohwow. You're right, Mello. This is way deep."

"This is totally like the verse I found last week," Harmony said. "I tried to memorize it. It's Jeremiah, for sure, but I'm not sure about the numbers. I'm thinking 29:11. 'For I know the plans I have for you ... plans to ...'" She stopped. "What's the rest? Something about help."

I smiled and finished the verse for her. "Plans to prosper you and not to harm you, plans to give you hope and a future."

Harmony looked surprised. "You know that verse?"

I looked up at the ceiling of the banya and took a big breath. "I know it, yeah. Living it is something else."

We sat quietly for a few minutes, watching the steam rise.

"Hey," I asked, "does that mean we aren't really going to Dobraykatooey or wherever it was?"

"Sī," Harmony answered. "I made all that up to teach you a lesson."

"I should beat you up," I said.

Harmony laughed. "Try it. You're forgetting I'm a blue belt in karate."

"It doesn't matter. I can't move," I said.

"No kidding," Mello agreed. "The banya is working wonders. I'm so relaxed I'm about to pass out. We should probably go back in the house."

"Can we pray first?" I asked quietly.

"*Bueno* idea," Harmony said, reaching for my hand. She bowed her head and prayed, "God, this trip has been cool frijoles. But it's also been hard. We don't know the language and we don't know what to expect from one minute to the next. Help us trust Pastor Kovitch and follow his lead. Help us relax and enjoy the days we have left. And help us trust you."

Mello added, "God, you are so good to let us come here. It's been just excellent. But we do need your help. It's stressful! Guide Pastor Kovitch as he makes plans for us. Help us follow his lead, and help us follow you."

I felt tears running down my face. At first when I opened my mouth, my voice didn't work. I cleared my throat and said, "God, my friends are right. It's hard for me to trust Pastor Kovitch. I want to be in control. But I can't. Help me let go." I took a deep breath. "Not just of the trip. I want you to take control of everything—my whole life. Amen."

Harmony and Mello threw their sweaty arms around me.

Mello said, "There has to be a song in this."

"I wish I had your talent for putting my feelings into words," I told her. "I'd love to be able to describe how I feel right now."

Mello closed her eyes and leaned against the wall for a minute.

"If only I knew what you help me to know," she said, "I would have been here a long time ago ..." Just in those first few words, I knew Mello's heart was totally about our next big song.

Harmony interrupted, "Wait, wait ... listen: Make me worthy of this journey. Pick me up so I can see where I been ain't where I'm going." And I knew we had a chorus and the bridge.

The three of us worked together until we had verses and a tune.

"We have got to go in and try this with instruments!" Harmony said.

I looked around the banya before we left. I wanted to remember it clearly — the place where I gave it all to God.

"So anyway, what do you think we'll do tomorrow?" Harmony asked as we opened the door and the cold air blasted over us.

I looked at her in amazement. Hadn't we just had an hour talk about that? I jabbed her with my elbow and said, "You are so, so lucky you are a blue belt."

chapter • 12

•••

Saturday

The next morning Sasha told all of us to load everything we brought to Russia into the van, and he took off driving. We finally stopped in front of a big building that looked like a school. A bus parked beside us.

Harmony said, "Look! It's the Russian choir!"

"Maybe they're doing the concert today," Mello said.

We climbed out of the van and I went to find Natalia. She laughed when she saw me and gave me a big hug. I pulled out my Russian-English dictionary and we started trying to talk.

Then Sasha walked up and said, "Verily, I say unto you, you should get your equipment set up."

"So the Chosen Girls are doing the concert?" I asked.

Sasha smiled. "Indeed, the Chosen Girls will do a concert with the Russian choir."

I wanted to panic. Our rock band and their classical choir? How would that work?

I told Natalia I had to go, and I went to the van to get my stuff. Harmony, Mello, Lamont, and Joel were there too. I said, "Hey, did you hear the news? We're doing this concert with the Russian choir."

Harmony said, "I don't see that working very well. We don't speak Russian. How can we do songs with them? Or do they do songs, then we do songs?"

"Or do we go first?" Mello asked. "And then they wrap it up?"

"Don't freak," I reminded them. "God's in charge. Let's talk to him about it, OK?"

We all grabbed hands. I prayed, "God, this day belongs to you, and we belong to you. We choose to trust you to make this concert what you want it to be. Amen." I said, "Let's set up and see what happens."

Once we were onstage and tuned up, Sasha came over with the choir director. "This is Nickolai Petrohvna. He leads the choir, and he wants very much we shall plan together today's concert."

I smiled at Nickolai. "Sweet. Let's plan."

Sasha said, "I am not sure why you say, 'sweet.' "

"*Har-ah-shor*," I corrected. "Good."

Sasha nodded and said, "Nickolai likes for the choir to sing first, maybe four songs."

We nodded.

"Then the Chosen Girls sing maybe three, and do the drama about prayer?"

We nodded again.

"And then he likes the choir to sing together with the Chosen Girls, the song you sing in Russian — the Lord's Prayer."

Harmony blurted, "Cool frijoles!"

Sasha asked, "What is this *frijoles*?"

"It means *beans* in Spanish," Mello said with a giggle.

"So you want cold beans?" Sasha asked. "I will check on that. I think we will not eat, though, until after the concert."

Harmony shot a look at Mello. "Don't confuse the poor guy," she said. Then she turned to Sasha. "*Cool frijoles* means *good*—har-ah-shor."

He smiled and said, "Oh, it becomes clear to me. So everyone is happy with the plan?"

We told him we were.

Sasha nodded and in his serious voice said, "Sweet. Sweet, cold beans!"

•••

We stayed backstage while the choir sang. Their music, of course, was way fabulous.

I had mixed feelings about being in the same concert as Natalia's group. I thought about my mom in the audience, wishing her daughter sang and dressed like the choir members. I whispered to Mello, "They make me feel kind of shallow or untalented or something."

Mello looked totally surprised. "No way! Are you forgetting God called you? He made you the way you are, Trin—from the songs he gives you down to the way you dress."

After the choir, Pastor Kovitch spoke to the audience for a while. Then he introduced us, and the crowd clapped so loud you'd have thought we were U2 or something.

During the first song, I kept looking at Natalia in the front row. I tried to stand up straight and tall, and sing in a little more professional voice. I toned down my guitar a lot too.

Harmony stared me down, but I just smiled at her and kept singing. After the song, she ran over to me while everyone clapped for us. "Please, Trin, the Chosen Girls are a rock band, not a classical choir. You're ruining everything."

Then she ran back to her place.

The next song was "You've Chosen Me." It's based partly on my life verse, John 15:16. I think about the verse every time we sing the song. The verse says, "You did not choose me, but I chose you and appointed you to go and bear fruit—fruit that will last. Then the Father will give you whatever you ask in my name."

When I moved to California, it helped so much to know God chose me. Maybe now God was using Natalia and the whole Russia trip to remind me that he chose me—*me*: loud, bossy, bold, pink-haired, rock-star Trin.

If I could trust him with my future, why couldn't I trust him to make me who he wanted me to be?

I smiled as I sang to him. I let my body move to the music, I let my voice soar, and I let it rip on my guitar. After the song I looked at Harmony. She gave me a thumbs-up. I felt like God was giving me a big thumbs-up too.

For our third song, we sang the new one we'd made up in the banya. We called it "Top of the World," and writing it had ripped all the way into my soul. The second verse was totally my own work and I loved how it summed up our whole Russia experience:

Doesn't it seem strange
How quickly things can change
When you're ready to open your heart.
I just can't keep it down.
Gotta shout it out.

Find more ways to give praise to you, God.
Help me to spread your word
Till every soul has heard,
'Cuz I wanna be here.
Yeah, I wanna come through
And I wanna reach out,
And I wanna be true.

I couldn't help smiling through the whole song.

Next we did the drama about the power of prayer. The adults surprised me by loving it as much as the kids at the orphanage had.

When the time came for the closing song, the choir filed back up onto the stage and stood on either side of us. We sang the Lord's Prayer in English the first time, then the choir sang it in Russian. We closed by singing it in Russian together. I couldn't believe how fabulous it sounded. I got chill bumps all over—singing in Russian with a Russian choir. Way cool.

After the concert, we gave away New Testaments again—hundreds of them. I hoped the people would actually go home and read them. I felt that same urge to tell them what a difference God can make. Could they understand enough from our concert?

When the last person in line had a Bible, Sasha hurried us back into the van. This time we followed the bus to another village. On the way, Sasha turned around and said, "Surely you can do the same thing once again, dah? Another concert with the choir?"

"Dah," I answered. "That will be sweet."

•••

The second concert went even better, maybe because I didn't compare myself to Natalia. And afterward some old people fed us. Ohwow, loads of food.

As I dug into my second helping of potatoes, Mello whispered, "Remember what Pastor Kovitch said about the food? That there's so much of it because of the radiation?"

I almost choked. Instead I swallowed, smiled, and said, "Another chance to trust God, huh?"

Harmony giggled and I looked at her. "Hey, this day is going just like you said it would, Harmony. Two concerts and a lunch. If we do another concert after this, I'll never believe you were making all that up."

Right then Sasha walked up. "Verily I say unto you, we have today one more event. You must make yourself ready to go."

Harmony laughed so hard, tea shot out her nose. Hot tea. When she could talk again she said, "It's a fluke, I promise. I really didn't know what we were doing. I still don't."

•••

Mello and Harmony fell asleep after lunch as the van bumped along the dirt roads. When we stopped, it looked like we were in the middle of nowhere.

"Sasha, are we back in the dead zone?" I asked as I climbed out.

He smiled. "Indeed, no, this is a place of much beauty," he answered.

The choir bus pulled in next to our van, and Natalia climbed out. She grabbed my hand and pulled me over a grassy hill, with everyone else following. On the other side, a huge banner said, in English, "Thank you, Chosen Girls!"

"Verily I say unto you," Sasha began, "the pastor wants we shall all gather beside the lake." He pointed to an area where a few people stood, waiting.

Joel said, "Hey! What's my dad doing here?"

"Look, Trin!" Harmony yelled. "There's your dad too!" Mom practically ran to him. They kissed, and then put their arms around each other. I snuck up behind Dad to give him a hug, but when I got close enough to hear Mom, I froze.

"You won't believe what Trin did on this trip," Mom said. *Uh-oh*, I thought. *Here comes the choir contest story.* "She made friends with a beautiful Russian girl named Natalia."

Oh. Not the contest, I thought, completely freaking out. *Mom's going to tell him all about Miss Perfect Natalia.* I shouldn't torture myself, but I couldn't help it. I plopped on a nearby blanket with a sigh, willing myself not to listen but unable to avoid it.

"She amazed me," Mom bubbled. "How could she reach out to someone she couldn't even communicate with? But you know our Trin. She had her little dictionary and gave it her best shot. I wish you could have seen her!"

I stared at my knees. Was she talking about me?

I amazed her?

"And onstage!" Mom went on. "Such a presence. I would have died to get up in front of maybe a thousand people in another country. But Trin just sings as if it's only her and God. It's beautiful. Jeff, I thought my heart would burst through my chest."

"She's quite a girl." That deep voice belonged to Joel's dad. "You've done a fine job raising her." I had to look up. And I blinked to make sure I was actually awake.

"Oh, thanks. But I certainly can't take the credit," Mom answered. "Trin's nothing like me. I wish I had her exuberance ... her charm. I'm a wallflower, myself."

"A very charming wallflower," Dad said, leaning down to kiss Mom on the forehead.

I stood up, wiped away a tear, and cleared my throat. "Enough smooching," I said. I pushed my way between Mom and Dad, looked up at Dad, and said, "It's so good to see you!"

"You too, Trin," Dad said as Pastor Kovitch clapped his hands together three times. Everyone got quiet and sat on blankets, logs, or large rocks. Joel, surprisingly, sat down right next to me.

Pastor Kovitch spoke to the crowd as Sasha repeated his speech in English.

Sasha translated, "When my friend told me an American rock band was coming, I felt nervous. I didn't know what kind of people they would be or what kind of message they would share. But I am so pleased that God led me to invite the Chosen Girls to Clinsky.

"This band has been a real help to our ministry. They brought medical supplies, which are a blessing to our local hospital. Some of the doctors and nurses who did not believe in God were very touched by this act of kindness from Christians.

"They brought toys to our orphans. When those children play with their new toys, they will remember the Chosen Girls. They will remember their music and the power of prayer.

"They drew people in — by the thousands — who would never have come to church to hear me preach. They shared the good news, and allowed us to share the good news as well."

The crowd burst into applause, and I didn't notice the tears streaming down my face until Joel grinned and wiped them away with his thumb.

"And most importantly," Sasha translated, "they handed out Bibles. The Word of God is living and active. It will change the lives of those who read it."

"I would like to read a letter a young woman brought by our church this morning." Pastor Kovitch pulled a sheet of paper out of an envelope and held it up for everyone to see. Then he read the letter aloud.

Sasha translated,

Pastor Kovitch,

I want to tell you what happened to me yesterday. I was out of hope and miserable when I wandered by the city hall. I heard rock music, and I remembered the American band was playing.

I love rock music, so I went inside. There weren't any empty seats, so I stood in the aisle.

The Americans onstage looked so happy. They didn't look like the rock stars I've seen on TV. I wondered what made them different.

I watched the lead singer—the girl with pink hair. She seemed very confident. And I knew enough English to know she was singing about God choosing her. I thought maybe that was what made her happy.

> At the end of the concert, I took a Bible. I started reading in Matthew, and I couldn't stop. I stayed awake most the night, reading.
>
> That's how I learned God has chosen me too. He sent his Son to die in my place, so I can belong to him.
>
> I found the address of the church in the front of the Bible, and I am going to bring you this letter. And on Sunday, I will come to church to learn more about the God who loves me.
>
> I wish you would please tell the Chosen Girls thank you for coming to Russia. Because of them, I now have hope.

Pastor Kovitch folded up the letter and put it back in the envelope. Then he pulled out a stack of envelopes and—while Sasha translated for us—said, "The letter I read is one of eighteen I have received since the Chosen Girls have been here. I'm sure there will be many more in the days to come." He looked right at us and said in Russian, "Spah-see-bah."

Our whole little group of Americans stood together later, talking about what an amazing good-bye party the Russians surprised us with.

"Thanks for letting Joel sit by you," Lamont whispered.

I looked at him in shock.

"Don't pretend you haven't noticed!" Lamont said. "He's tried to get near you this whole week."

"Me?" I asked. *"Me?"*

Mello interrupted us. "Um, what's Pastor Kovitch doing?"

We looked at him. He bent over and put his hand down, then stood up and held it out. Then he did it again. And again.

"He's finally cracked," Harmony whispered. "I think you put him over the edge, Trin."

"Me?" I asked. "Maybe the whole tour. The pressure of lining up all those concerts. Or maybe—ohwow—I bet it's the radiation! It finally got to be too much!" I looked at him and said, "I wonder if this can be reversed? What if we could get him to the States?"

Mrs. Kovitch looked at her husband, but she didn't look worried. She just smiled and held one fist up in front of her mouth. Then she started moving her lips, but no sound came out. She swayed back and forth.

"*No es bueno!*" Harmony cried. "They've both gone *loco*. I guess we can be glad this didn't happen days ago."

"But we can't just leave them like this," I said. "They have a child to take care of. Ohwow, does 9-1-1 work in Russia?"

Mello shook her head and smiled.

I looked at her in shock. "What are you smiling about? There is nothing happy about two wonderful people losing their mental abilities because they've chosen to serve God in a radiation-infested part of Russia."

"No, but there is something happy about two Russians thanking us for handing out Bibles and singing," Mello answered.

I looked back at Pastor Kovitch bending over, reaching down, and holding his hand out.

Then I looked at his wife holding her fist by her lips, mouthing words and swaying back and forth.

They smiled at us and said, "Spah-see-bah!"

Oh. I guess pantomime was *their* way of overcoming the language barrier too.

"Well, that's a relief!" I said. I smiled at them and said, "Pah-zhahl-oos-tah."

Sasha came over to say good-bye, and I freaked. I didn't have a good-bye gift. I ran back to the van, found my suit-case and dug around in it. I didn't have much left. Then my eyes fell on my Bible. It's a New International Version. Way easier than King James.

I pulled it out and flipped through it. I'd underlined all my favorite verses in it. Some of them had notes and dates in the margins — times God showed me something big. The most recent ones were from this trip. I bit my lip. Did I really want to let it go? I took a big breath and knew it was right.

I walked back over the hill and handed Sasha my favorite Bible.

"Hey, Sasha, I love the way you say 'verily' and 'unto you,' but if you want a Bible that sounds more like the way Americans talk, you might try this one."

He looked at the cover and read, "New International Version. I say unto you, Trin, I shall try to find one of these. I have noticed that the Chosen Girls do not speak in the same way I do, and I want to improve my English. Thank you for your suggestion, but I do not have a gift unto you." He tried to hand it back.

I shook my head and pushed it back into his hands. "Your English is fine, Sasha, and your gift was driving us every-where and telling us what everyone said. But this is my Bible, and I've marked my favorite parts. I want you to have it, to remember me by."

His eyes got misty. He opened the Bible and looked through it. "Spah-see-bah," he finally whispered. Then he looked up and smiled and said "Ohwow, this is sweet, dah?"

I smiled back and said, "Verily."

When Sasha told us to get back in the van, I totally lost it. I hugged Natalia and cried my head off. I felt like an idiot—I had only known her for a few days. She kept saying, "Heaven," and pointing to the sky, then to me and her. That made me cry even harder—the sadness of knowing how long it would be until I'd see her again, and the sweetness of knowing I absolutely would see her again. And the next time, we would be able to understand each other, forever!

I got in the van and sat on something lumpy.

"Wait!" I yelled at Pastor Kovitch, who had already started the van. "I forgot!"

It was my pink nubby sweater—the one Natalia loved. I ran to the bus and banged on the windows, asking for her.

She finally came out, and I handed her the sweater. She started crying and talking to me in Russian. I think she felt bad about not having a gift for me. I shook my head and tried to tell her it didn't matter.

Then she smiled real big and put her hands behind her neck. She undid the cross necklace she had on, and reclasped it on me.

One last hug, and I ran back to the van. As we drove away, I put my hand to my chest and wrapped it around the crucifix that dangled there.

In Russia I learned about letting go . . . but the cross?

That's the one thing I'll always hang on to.

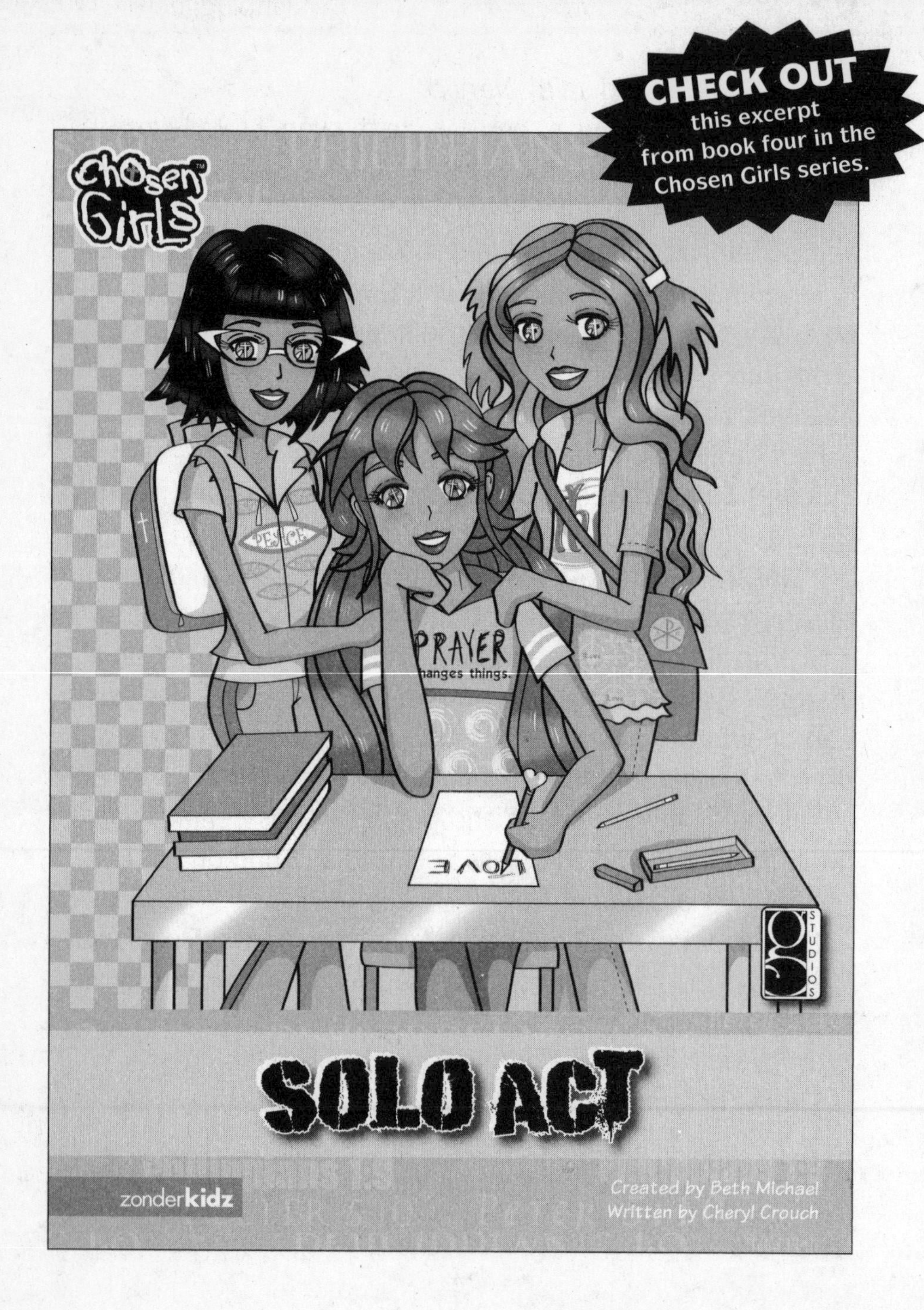
CHECK OUT
this excerpt
from book four in the
Chosen Girls series.
Chosen Girls
PRAYER
changes things.
LOVE
g STUDIOS
SOLO ACT
zonderkidz
Created by Beth Michael
Written by Cheryl Crouch

chapter • 1

• • •

Thursday

My life used to be simple. All I needed: a good book and my fluffy fleece blanket.

Then everything changed with the Trinvasion. Since Trin Adams moved here and took over our lives, my best friend Harmony and I have never been the same.

Sure, I'm glad Trin talked us into being a rock band. I'm a real drummer now. But I don't like being out front, even though I can do it. Thankfully, I won't have to worry about that for a while.

Now summer's here, school's over, and my only scheduled gig is going to Surf & Sand City, where Harmony and I spend a week every year—huge cliffs overlooking the ocean, tons of cute boys, and time to read and do a whole bunch of nothing.

But best of all, no band, no work, and no Trin . . .

• • •

I had just rolled into my softest fleece throw and shuffled to my bookshelf to choose a book when my cell phone rang "La Bamba."

"Harmony?"

"Hello, Mello!" Harmony's voice blasted out at me. "Are you packed?"

"Packing."

"I knew it. Are you ready for some serious fun-o-rama?"

"I'm ready for some rest-o-rama, Harmony — picking out a novel as we speak."

I could practically hear her rolling her eyes.

"You've got to be the only teenager in Southern California who thinks a retreat at Surf & Sand City is about resting," she accused.

"You can do whatever you want," I answered. "You'll know where to find me."

"On your favorite cliff, reading a book," she said in her most disgusted voice.

I closed my eyes and pictured it. I could almost smell the ocean and feel the breeze. "Definitely."

"I can't believe we leave tomorrow. One o'clock, just like last year?"

"Definitely."

"And you signed us up to room together, right?"

"Definitely."

"Hasta mañana!"

I punched the End button on my phone. Before I even put it down, it rang again. But it wasn't "La Bamba."

"Hello?"

"May I please speak to Mello McMann?"

"This is she," I answered.

"Mello, this is David Karuthers. You know that I'm coordinating this year's retreat. Today I'm pulling together last-minute details at the office. Are you coming to choir practice tonight?" he asked in his bouncy voice.

"Yes," I answered, trying to figure out what choir had to do with anything.

"Do you think your friend Harmony could come with you? And maybe you could come early? I'd like to speak to the two of you about the trip."

I paused before I answered. Was this about last year's retreat? The speaker's shoes hot-glued to the ceiling? Or the toothpaste on the pillows? Or maybe the water-balloon launcher?

If so, he needed to talk to Harmony, not me. Maybe it wasn't the best idea to invite her to join my youth group on this trip every year.

I said, "I think so. I'll call Harmony."

"Great. Meet me at the youth center at six thirty."

• • •

"If I was going to get in trouble for that stuff, don't you think it would have happened last year?" Harmony whispered as we walked up the church sidewalk.

I shrugged. "Maybe they found out something new. Maybe someone just now complained. How should I know?"

"So why do you have to be here? All you did last year was read."

I threw an arm around Harmony's shoulder. "I guess I'm guilty by association," I said with a groan.

We found Mr. Karuthers inside the youth center. He didn't look mad at all. He smiled real wide, bounced over to some chairs, and pulled three of them into a triangle.

"Here, girls, have a seat," he said. "Thanks for coming."

I looked at Harmony, and she raised her eyebrows. So far, so good.

"Mello, Harmony, I want this retreat to be a special time for everyone who attends. I know it's a good time to relax, but I think it should be more than that."

Harmony shot me a look. I felt like saying, "I don't think he's talking about pranks and water-balloon fights."

"Last night I went down the list of students who will be attending," he continued. "When I got to your names, I knew I had the answer I've been looking for!"

My heart started beating out a warning. I didn't want to be anyone's answer to anything. I wanted to hide on my cliff and read.

He smiled at us and asked, "How would the Chosen Girls like to do an outreach concert on the beach Saturday night?"

"Cool frijoles!" Harmony said, probably as much from relief about not being in trouble as from excitement about the concert.

I tried to process. One concert wouldn't be such a big deal. I would only lose one evening of downtime. But I would have to bring my drums. And Trin.

It wasn't what I had planned on.

Mr. Karuthers talked on and on about how all the campers could pass out flyers Friday. Loads of people would come. He said the concert would be a great opportunity for people to hear the positive message our band loved to share.

I started simmering inside. *I don't care if those people hear our message, Mr. Karuthers. I want to read my book, not do a concert.*

But I smiled and said, "Definitely, Mr. Karuthers. We'll check with Trin, but I'm sure she'll say yes. Can our soundman come too?"

• • •

Lamont agreed immediately, offering to help with more than sound. He'd always wanted to go to Surf & Sand City. And Trin definitely said yes. Actually, she screamed, "Ohwow! Yes! Sweet! I can't wait! What should I pack?"

I knew Trin had been feeling left out since Harmony and I had planned to go without her. I finished packing and spent the rest of the night chatting online.

Trin: *ohwow—it's right on the beach?*

Harmony: *sí. muy bonita. bring sunscreen.*

Trin: *sand volleyball?*

Me: *n surfing lessons, horses, mountain biking*

Harmony: *LOL! like mello ever did any of that b4!!! but u will luv it, trin—just wait til u c the cabins. way cute*

Trin: *i can't wait. i just have 2 learn 2 surf!*

Lamont: *i haven't been on a board in months*

Me: *thx for the warning—we'll stay out of ur way*

Trin: *how many pairs of shoes r u bringing?*

Me: *2*

Lamont: *what does THAT matter?*

Harmony: *be quiet, Lamont. i packed 5*

Trin: *i think i can make it with 8*

Lamont: *we're only there a week. why do u need 8 pairs of shoes?*

Trin: *didn't some1 tell u 2 b quiet?*

I could see Harmony was psyched about Trin's going. Now she'd have someone to hang with. I should have been happy for her, since I just wanted to kick back. But instead I felt irritated.

• • •

Friday Morning

Friday morning we met early at the shed behind my house. Harmony and I had used the shed as a playhouse for years, but now it serves as a studio. We needed to run through the songs and make sure we were all cool with the plan. Lamont joined us, since he lives right next door.

I did some rolls on the snare to warm up. Harmony got out her bass, and Trin started tuning her electric. I asked what song we should start with.

Trin looked past me, smiled her hugest smile, and said, "I can just imagine pounding to the edge of a cliff on the back of a black stallion, overlooking the Pacific Ocean— "

"Just don't run over Mello. She'll be sitting on that cliff, reading," Harmony said.

I shook my head. "If we don't get started, I'll never get to chill. We'll be practicing the whole time."

"Should I bring the camera?" Lamont asked. "I can tape the concert."

"A concert on the beach!" Harmony said. "It might be our biggest one yet. Sī, tape it!"

"But in order to do a concert, we'll have to know what song we're opening with," I reminded them. "Which brings us back to why we're here this— "

"Are we changing to superhero suits halfway through?" Harmony interrupted.

"Wait! I forgot to pack mine!" Trin said, already walking across the room. "And my white boots. Ohwow, I better go right now." She packed her guitar into the case. "And I forgot bracelets! I so am not good with last-minute packing."

"You definitely should do the super suits," Lamont said. "That's your trademark. It's what makes the Chosen Girls stand out. Either super suits or chicken suits."

Harmony whirled to face him. "The chicken disaster is over. Do not mention the chicken suits, the chicken concert, or the chicken jingle unless you want me to practice my newest karate move on you."

Lamont shut his mouth, but he started humming the tune for *Chik'n Quik / Chicken on a stick / It's so yummy for your tummy /Everybody loves Chik'n Quik*.

Harmony put her guitar on the couch and raised her arms to fighting position.

"You didn't say I couldn't hum!" Lamont cried, crossing his arms in front of his face in self-defense.

"What about our practice?" I asked Trin. "We didn't even run through one song."

"We'll have to do it when we get there," she said as she ran out the door. "See you at one!"

Harmony put her arms down, and Lamont sighed in mock relief. She grabbed her bass, put it in the case, and fastened the latches. "Know what? I forgot my new bracelets too!" she said. "And I think I should take my purple flip-flops." She moved toward the door.

"Harmony," I whined. "I don't want to spend the whole time we're there practicing for the concert."

She looked back at me. "Don't worry, Mello. We'll be fine," she said. Then she left too.

I looked at Lamont. "Please don't tell me you need to pack bracelets or flip-flops," I begged him.

He shrugged. "Nope. But I do need to get my camera and the charger and— "

"Fine!" I said. "Just go."

He walked toward the door and said, "Mello, the concert will be great. The Chosen Girls can do this with their eyes closed. What's wrong with you?"

I shook my head. I did know one thing—now that the Chosen Girls were officially involved, this retreat would be anything but downtime.

zonder**kidz**

Chosen Girls is a dynamic new series that communicates a message of empowerment and hope to Christian youth who want to live out their faith. These courageous and compelling girls stand for their beliefs and encourage others to do the same. When their cross-cultural outreach band takes off, Trinity, Melody, and Harmony explode onto the scene with style, hot music, and genuine, age-relatable content.

Backstage Pass

Book One • Softcover • ISBN 0-310-71267-X

In *Backstage Pass,* shy, reserved Melody gets her world rocked when a new girl moves in across the street from her best friend, Harmony. Soon downtime—or any time with Harmony at all—looks like a thing of the past as the strong-willed Trinity invades Melody and Harmony's world and insists that the three start a rock band.

Available now at your local bookstore!

zonder**kidz**

Big Break

Book Five • Softcover • ISBN 0-310-71271-8

The Chosen Girls are back! As opportunities for the band continue to grow, Harmony can't resist what she sees as a big break ... and what could be better than getting signed by an agent?

Sold Out

Book Six • Softcover • ISBN 0-310-71272-6

Dedicated to proving herself to others, Trinity gets involved in organizing the school talent show. Before she knows it, she accepts a dare from Chosen Girls' rival band to be decided by the outcome of a commericial audition.

Available November 2007 at your local bookstore!

Available November 2007 at your local bookstore!

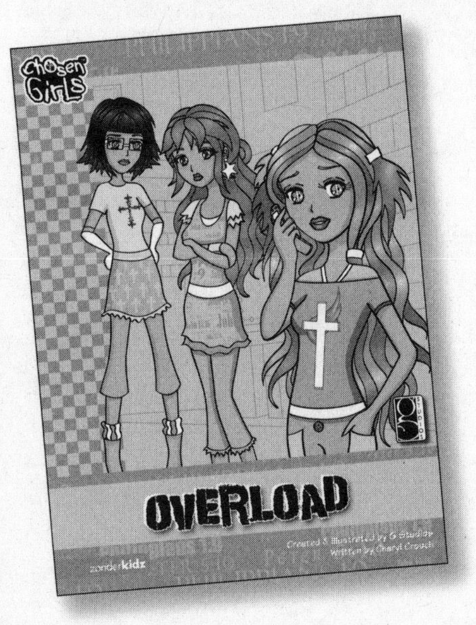

Overload

Book Seven • Softcover • ISBN 0-310-71273-4

Melody discovers a latent talent for leadership that she never knew she had. When she begins a grief recovery group for kids like her, she loses her focus on the work God is doing through the Chosen Girls.

Reality Tour

Book Eight • Softcover • ISBN 0-310-71274-2

When the Chosen Girls go on their first multi-city tour in a borrowed RV, Harmony's messiness almost spoils their final show. What's worse, she almost blows her opportunity to witness to her cousin Lucinda.

zonder**kidz**

zonder**kidz**

We want to hear from you. Please send your comments about this book to us in care of zreview@zondervan.com. Thank you.

Grand Rapids, MI 49530
www.zonderkidz.com

ZONDERVAN.com/
AUTHORTRACKER
follow your favorite authors